ELEVATOR PEOPLE

CHARLOTTE LAWS

For information about this title or to order other books and/or electronic media, contact the publisher or author.

Stroud House Publishing
Offices in NY and CA

ISBNs:
978-0-9961335-0-0 (Print)
978-1-7333410-0-4 (eBooks)

Printed in the United States of America

"Elevator People is a brand-new idea. It is a rich and layered exploration of the human condition. Great world-building. Compelling and thought-provoking."

– Kaijah Greenwood, author.

"Wow! An extremely imaginative and enjoyable story!"

– Christopher Coates, author.

"Bubbling with wit and wisdom! Charlotte Laws's Elevator People is a twisty gem and remarkably original!"

– Richard Riis, author.

*To my granddaughters, Atlas and Blake, who
are destined to lead compassionate lives.
I love you.*

Contents

Characters and Terminology

Agent Bones – Manager of the Earthling Extermination Project.

Angus Van Graff – Arrogant. Rich kid. Keiko's Brother. 25. Elevator Person.

Anna Green – Activist. 20.

Bailey Iverson – Single mom. 19. Elevator Person.

Bernie Cruz – Former honor student. Has tattoos. 25. Elevator Person.

Carl Fox – Head of an NGO. Ex-military. 72. Elevator Person.

Darkon – Member of the Council of the Universe.

Detective Julie Ponderosa – Baltimore police detective.

Dr. Leila Dijon – Head researcher at the Worthington Research Institute.

Elevator people – People who disappeared from elevators in 2025.

Ellen Garcia – Head of an NGO. Buddhist. 62. Elevator Person.

Hal – Roger's childhood word for "hallucination." ("A man named Hal.")

Harry – Shirtless vagrant.

Henry – Barefoot vagrant.

Joan Adams – Roger Adams's wife. Real estate agent.

JP – Manager of Happy Farms.

Kara Carson – Female lead. Highly intelligent. 35. Elevator Person.

Keiko Van Graff – Angus's brother. 23. Elevator Person.

Luddite – A person opposed to new technology and progress.

Magistrate – President of the Council of the Universe.

Miles Sousa – Techie. 41.

Miss Pringles – Female miniature pig.

Mother Teresas – Derogatory nickname for Angus and Keiko.

Mr. Pebblebrook – Owner of the Paradise Mattress store.

Olive – Researcher at the Worthington Research Institute.

Randolph Schmidt – First Street Deli owner.

Roger Adams – Male lead. Head of an NGO. 45. Elevator Person.

Sammy – Male miniature pig.

Sheldon – Member of the Council of the Universe.

Vate – Slang term for an "elevator person."

Wrecks – People who oppose technology.

Chapter One

DILEMMAS

Agent Bones was a moral mosquito, buzzing into conversations with a judgy tongue and a bug-like stare. But he was an affable fellow who had befriended many particles in the universe. "Particle" was the word used to describe living beings, except on a judgment day, when it was customary to use the vernacular of the "planet under review."

Today was such a day: it was a pivotal moment for introducing resolutions, voting, arriving at a verdict, and selecting a supervisor to carry forth the official decree.

The Council of the Universe—the decider of all things pressing—was in session, determining the fate of an unremarkable but out-of-control planet called Earth. Terms such as "earthling," "people," "peril," and "destruction" were batted about. English was the most common mode of communication for business dealings on the third planet from the sun, so the council was required to converse in that language.

The chamber was commanding with an untamable echo and adorned with splashy marble floors, chair rails, dentil crown moldings, and a ceiling resembling a yacht's inverted hull. Swank gold plaques dotted the walls; each was engraved with the name of a different country on Earth. The magistrate and the other six council members sat behind a stately wooden judge's bench, which spanned the width of the room. It was emblazoned with the words "Council of the Universe." Hundreds of spectators sat in the audience section of the chamber, eagerly observing the proceedings. In addition, there were underlings who served as council aides flitting about and a handful of onlookers collected at the back of the room.

Agent Bones—typically called "Bones"—stood in the rear, buffing his snout with a nail file, intent on sanding away the rough spots. He looked much the same as the other beings in the room. He had human-like eyes and mouth, a platypus-shaped nose, ears like a bat, facial coloring like a raccoon, whiskers like a sea otter, a thick lion's mane, hairy legs, and floppy feet shaped like those of a kangaroo. His arms and hands resembled an ordinary man from Earth, but they sprouted out from a metallic "Tin Man" torso.

Bones held the prestigious title of "agent" for one reason: he was the brother-in-law of the cousin of the council's magistrate. Bones had attended dozens of proceedings for all sorts of planets and witnessed all sorts of outcomes, but this was his first experience related to Earth. He found meetings to be dull and long-winded. To pass the time, he focused on personal grooming. But primping was more than a distraction. For him, it was a joyous fixation.

"Your snout looks a little craggy," Bones whispered to the male particle on his left. "And there's a hair on your chin."

"Worry about yourself, Bones," the particle replied with a smile. "I'm not your project."

"Sorry." Bones hit himself with the nail file several times in a gesture of self-reproach.

The magistrate, a commanding female particle, spoke into the microphone. "Earth has become a calamitous force, causing hurricanes, tornadoes, monsoons, blizzards, earthquakes, and drought throughout the universe. If it is allowed to continue, 32,000 planets will be dead within a year. Today, we will be voting on how to handle this wretched orb. Think about the best way to exterminate Earth's ugly little people, because anything less is not an option."

Darkon, the most menacing particle on the council, replied, "Let's just blow it up. Bye-bye, stinky little mothball."

"Darkon, that's impractical," the magistrate shot back. "Abrupt action would assure the annihilation of millions of planets. Not thousands. We must exterminate in a surgical and methodical way. We must be calculated and rational."

Sheldon, the most sympathetic particle on the council, said in a meek tone, "We could ask the people on Earth to change."

Laughter erupted in the chamber.

The magistrate rolled her eyes. "Sorry, Sheldon. We're not trying that again."

Darkon mumbled, "Sheldon's such a simpleminded cell."

"I don't really like the idea of torture," Sheldon added.

Darkon countered, "Yet, you torture us with your presence at every meeting."

"Please, no personal attacks." The magistrate wrote numbers at breakneck speed on a large board that suddenly materialized and appeared to float in the air. It would have looked like gibberish to humans, but the particles in the room seemed to understand the significance of the data. Each figure, number, and symbol vanished one second after it was scrawled.

The magistrate continued, "I believe I've come up with a solution. This is a rough draft of my proposal. Phase One will include a manipulation of the earthlings so we can conduct research. The results could prove valuable in the future if other planets go rogue. Then we move on to Phase Two, which includes a tiered liquidation."

Most particles nodded while fixated on the magical board, which then disappeared in its entirety.

"Before I delve into the details, I'd like to choose a director for this initiative," the magistrate said.

Dozens of particles oohed and aahed with raised hands.

"This will be called 'The Earthling Extermination Project,'" the magistrate continued. "And I'd like to appoint someone who has never been in a management role."

All hands came down because they had acted as supervisors in the past.

"We must bring newbies into the fold," the magistrate added. "Agent Bones will be the director of this project. My cousin recommends him. Agent Bones, are you present? Agent Bones, where are you?"

Although he wanted to slither into the air vent, Bones tentatively stepped forward.

"There you are." The magistrate smiled. "Come on. Come up to the front. Don't be shy."

Bones did as he was instructed.

"I'm not a good choice," Bones said. "I haven't had training."

"Everyone must get their hands bloody at some point." The magistrate grinned.

"Yes, ma'am."

"Mostly, you will supervise the initiative and communicate

with the earthlings. We, the council, make the decisions. You will carry forth our orders. Understand?"

"Yes, ma'am."

"Will you be able to uphold our extermination orders?"

"Well, they *have* been really immoral on Earth—"

The magistrate interrupted, "This is not about morality."

"Yes, ma'am."

"You may take your seat, Agent Bones, while the council and I vote on the particulars of the project."

"Yes, ma'am." Bones slid into an empty chair, trying to conceal his queasiness. He imagined he was on the precipice of an emotional black hole.

◈

Meanwhile, on planet Earth, at a well-stocked perfume laboratory in Baltimore, Maryland, Dr. Kara Carson hopped off a treadmill, drenched in sweat. She was a stunning woman with honey-colored skin; she wore yoga pants and a sports bra. Her tousled curls were arranged in a messy bun. She took a sterile sponge from a glass bowl and carefully wiped perspiration from her neck and underarms. Then she placed the moistened sponge in a beaker filled with all sorts of fragrance-making substances, such as musk, oud, vetiver, alcohol, dried herbs, bergamot, and flowers.

"Armpit Delite or The Pit of Passion. Not sure which is better." Kara's assistant laughed. She sat on a metal lab table, pumping her legs like a child on a swing.

"It would be called 'Axilla's Passion,'" Kara countered.

"What?"

"Axilla's the technical word for armpit. It comes from Latin."

"You're such a nerd." The assistant smiled.

The cream-colored room was spotless; display cases encased

it like a protective shell. The shelves held bottles and beakers, many of which were labeled.

A sign on the wall read "Bright Perfume Company." There was a sink, a microwave, scales, a refrigerator, funnels, atomizer spray nozzles, strainers, nitrile gloves, glass stirs, a clock on the wall, and lighting that illuminated the space at the recommended 750 lux. The treadmill looked out of place, but Kara wrote it off on her tax returns as a "research aid." She was determined to devise a pheromone perfume that would allure even the most aloof gentleman caller.

Before getting down to the business of science, Kara donned her white lab coat because she felt experiments needed to be conducted in a professional manner, not in gym clothes. She placed a lid on the beaker and carefully swirled the liquid like a glass of Chardonnay.

"You think it'll work this time?" The assistant jumped off the table. "I mean, saliva was not exactly a roaring success."

"Science is about trial and error."

"You could try urine or blood. They have pheromones, too."

Kara ignored the revolting comment.

"Who you gonna try it on? That cute fireman or maybe that curly-headed dude who works at the courthouse?"

"I thought I'd wear it tonight."

"Oh yeah. Roger will be at the gala." The assistant fetched a Coke from the refrigerator. "But he's married like the others. Right?"

"I'm lying in wait," Kara replied. "On pause. Idling in the wings. He might get divorced someday. You never know."

"You should be going out on the town every night, not being a homebody. And you shouldn't want leftovers."

Kara poured coumarin, a cinnamon-like substance, into a vial. "The beauty about getting older is your list of possible husbands expands. When I was twenty, there was only one guy I liked. When I was twenty-five, there were two. Now I'm thirty-five, and there are five."

"But they're all married." The assistant downed her soft drink.

"Forty-one percent of all marriages end in divorce. Since I have five potential suitors, according to statistics, there is a 92.85 percent chance that one of these men will eventually be single. I just have to wait it out." Kara used a dropper to take some liquid from the vial and examine it under a microscope.

The assistant glanced at the clock, which read four-thirty. "Well, I'm heading home. I'm not gonna argue with a professional spinster. Have fun tonight."

She left.

Kara placed some of her pheromone solution in a small container, screwed on the lid, and slipped it into her purse. She put the rest in the fridge, grabbed her coat, and headed home.

At her condo, Kara prepared for the evening's nonprofit gala, painting her toenails and touching up her makeup while listening to the song "In the Year 2525" by Zager and Evans. Her apartment represented the style of "cozy casual," yet it was filled with ceramic Foo Dogs and other spiritual figurines, giving it a more formal vibe.

A Harvard Medical School degree hung on the wall, as well as a certificate acknowledging Dr. Kara Carson as the director of the Middle East Poverty Foundation for Women and Girls. There were also impromptu photos of Kara posing next to poverty-stricken children from Syria and Kuwait. She was proud of her volunteer work; it was more fulfilling than carrying out her duties as a scent scientist.

The phone rang. Caller ID identified it as "Beelzebub"—Kara's secret name for the spiteful and catty womb-bearing beast who had brought her into the world.

"Hello, Mom. Did you need something?"

"I'm just calling to let you know I bought a new car. A navy Mercedes with a sunroof and ambient lighting."

"Great, Mom. I'm happy for you."

"Are you still driving that old Toyota?"

"Yep." Kara rifled through her closet in search of a dress for the evening's affair.

"That's a shame. You could be a neurosurgeon at the Mayo Clinic. But no. You work at The Cologne Depot."

"It's not cologne. It's perfume, and it's important work."

"No. It isn't. Perfume causes asthma. It leads to respiratory problems. Instead of healing people, you're making them sick. Your father was a respected cardiologist. The president even came to his funeral."

"I know, Mom."

"So, why don't you drop this nonsense and become a real doctor? You have the credentials."

"I don't like the sight of blood." Kara tossed a sexy black dress on the bed and stared at it fondly.

"That's like an accountant saying he doesn't like numbers. Or a writer saying she's allergic to paper. You're a ridiculous child."

"Anyway, I have a big event tonight, Mom. Gotta go. Congratulations on your new sunroof. I'm sure the ambient lighting will make you look ten years younger."

Kara ended the call and placed her lucky red scarf next to the black dress on her bed. It was embroidered with the words "To Kara, our warrior. From your little lambs." She smiled lovingly at the inscription.

※

She'd had thirty-two daydreams and eight nighttime dreams about Roger Adams since she first ran into him at a function five years prior. In other words, Kara had consciously and subconsciously cast him as the target of her affection.

Roger was forty-five, likable, attractive, and reliable, but a tad bland. When it came to ideas, he was the most boilerplate human alive. If he'd been on an actual plate, he would have been sliced white bread. He'd be the kind of food served to prisoners: not spicy, but filling.

His personality was similar; it was middle-of-the-road. He had the spunk of the solid yellow line on the Baltimore Beltway and the spontaneity of asphalt. Roger was, in a word, safe. He never veered from life's paint-by-numbers kit. His blueprint for existence was filled with ordinary thoughts and the desire to conform to society. He always tried to be considerate and appropriate. Most people deemed him polite but forgettable. Kara was not like most people: She viewed him as ruggedly handsome, witty, good-hearted, and fascinating.

Roger headed an organization called Environmental Action. The group was so influential in the community that Roger was regularly asked to host the annual nonprofit gala. The bash, which would be held that evening, honored charities in the region. It was a must-attend for prominent and mom-and-pop media outlets from New York City to Washington, D.C.

∽

Roger finished work and parked in the driveway of his Baltimore smart home. He noticed a real estate sign belonging to his wife, Joan, in the next-door neighbor's yard. Joan was the listing agent for this sale and had represented three properties on the street within the past few years.

At the front door of his tech-fortified house, Roger spoke loudly and clearly. "Open front door."

He placed his smartphone next to the knob, and clickety-click, the door unlocked.

He entered and used his voice to turn on the smart lights as he traversed from room to room. "Living room lights," "Dining room lights," "Kitchen lights."

The areas illuminated as expected. But when the kitchen bulbs came on, Roger found himself cheek to cheek with Joan, who appeared on a large wall-mounted monitor. It looked creepy, as if she was spying on him.

"Oh. You scared me," Roger said.

"Honey, could you come next door? I need some advice."

"Okay." Roger shut off the monitor.

He glanced around at the vast number of sticky notes attached to every conceivable surface: cabinets, drawers, the fridge, and even the windowsill. Joan had lists for meal ingredients, errands to be run, and chores for her husband to complete. She had a catalog of award-winning movies, the best restaurants in town, and the number of calories in her favorite foods. Roger sometimes called her "Post-it Joan." She had been obsessed with sticky notes since they tied the knot. Lists made the otherwise sleek, architectural dwelling look tacky.

Roger ventured back to the front door, where he recited his usual command. "Open front door."

The door replied, "Error."

Roger furrowed his brow, mumbling, "Why are there always glitches with this thing?" Then he stood tall and spoke clearly, "Open front door."

The door responded, "Error."

"Bypass error." Roger tried to contain his frustration.

"Password, please," the door retorted.

"Oh, crap. 9799?"

"Wrong password."

"9788?"

"Wrong password."

Roger yanked on the doorknob, but it would not budge. He screamed, "Let me out of here. Let me out of here."

The door snapped back, "Burglar. Burglar. Burglar…"

The word was repeated nonstop as Roger scrambled into the bedroom to search for the code.

"Bedroom lights on." The table lamps lit up, and Roger rummaged through the dresser. After searching under his socks and T-shirts, he ventured to Joan's side of the bureau. He opened her bra drawer and found a list identifying passwords for the bank, wi-fi, social media accounts, and the front door, among others.

Roger also caught a glimpse of something else, something he was clearly not supposed to see. Tucked under her lingerie were two more notes. One was titled "Javier's favorite bras," and the list began with "red lace luxury" and went on to mention a "yellow bra with hearts" and the "blue naughty girl peek-a-boo bra."

The second note he found was a to-do list for that year. "Divorce my boring husband" was the first entry; "Marry Javier" was the second entry. Next to the notes were photos of Joan with a muscular man in a Speedo, whom Roger assumed to be Javier. They appeared to be at a hotel pool.

Roger was shocked, devastated, and unable to breathe. He leaned against the dresser for support as he felt his legs get weak.

Questions darted through his mind. *How could Joan feel this way? Why didn't she say anything? How long has she thought of me as boring? Was Javier her only lover? How long had the affair been going on?*

Roger stumbled back to the front door with the password in hand. His confusion and distress had grown into rage as he blurted out the code "9798." The door unlocked with a loud click.

Roger yelled at the door, "Thanks, asshole."

The door replied, "You're welcome, Mrs. Adams."

Roger marched next door, where he found Joan standing beside the seller in the front yard adjacent to a muddy hole in the grass. A truck, emblazoned with the words "AAA Staging Company," was parked on the street, and two men were carrying a sofa into the listing.

"Staging will help it sell." Joan grinned at the seller.

The seller replied, "It's expensive. I hope I'm not gonna get a bunch of looky-loos who waste my time. I've heard that saying in your industry: 'Buyers are liars. Sellers are yellers.'"

"That saying's just a joke. We agents love buyers and sellers. And you're certainly not a yeller."

"So, what do you want?" Roger confronted his wife, ramming the question down her throat.

Bewildered by his ire, she spoke to the seller, "Sometimes he has a bad day at work." Then she directed her words to her husband and pointed at the wet hole in the grass. "Is this a sewer leak?"

"How would I know?"

"You used to be an environmental inspector. You should know about these things."

"I wasn't a sewer technician, but it looks like a sewer leak."

Joan and the seller seemed disappointed. "I'll call the plumber now," the seller announced as he headed toward his home.

"Is that it?" Roger blasted Joan.

"Yeah. What's the matter with you?"

"I need to speak with you in private. It's important."

Joan looked perplexed, and then checked the calendar on her smartphone. "We could talk on Thursday morning before you go to work. I could carve out fifteen minutes."

This response left Roger feeling even more apoplectic. But he repressed his feelings, nodded coldly, and stomped back to his house. Part of him wished he had embarrassed his cheating wife in front of her client, but another part did not want to blow the sale because they needed the commission to help cover the mortgage.

It was an hour later. Joan sat on the couch watching a cable news show that featured two political pundits and a host. Roger stood behind her in the bedroom doorway peering at the television while slipping on his jacket.

The first pundit said, "Political divisiveness has reached a breaking point. The people in your party are slaves to misinformation and conspiracy theories."

The second pundit shot back, "We're the slaves? Your side's a bunch of robots, marching to the beat of the establishment. Your party's trying to control society with censorship and a cultlike obedience."

The host of the show responded, "The ideological future of America is clearly uncertain."

Roger passed through the living room in his designer business suit and an eye-catching tie; he was ready to head over to the Zelles Hotel for the splashy gala.

"When will you be home?" Joan asked.

"Around eleven." He spoke in a mechanical way, sounding a little like the front door.

During the drive to the gala, Roger questioned his life and identity. He vowed, then and there, to change his predictable behavior, to stop being boring, to no longer be vanilla. He figured that day might mark a tipping point or translate into an epiphany. He was hell-bent on metamorphosing into a bold and spontaneous man.

Roger also thought about his job. If his marriage had been a sham, maybe his whole life had been a sham. Part of him wanted to start over, get a fresh start, maybe even abandon his executive directorship at Environmental Action. He'd always wanted to take up snowboarding and manage a ski shop.

Maybe he could move to Switzerland. Of course, another part of him wanted to beat Javier into prune pulp and steal his wife back. Unfortunately, he still loved the hussy. But could he forgive her?

Roger was filled with rage and jealousy, but he knew he needed to set aside his hostility and compartmentalize for the next few hours. He needed to put Joan out of his mind. It would be unprofessional to let his personal situation disrupt the event. He was the host, and it was his duty to be focused, civil, and sociable—to do the best possible job.

&

The entrance of the Zelles Hotel was hopping. There were guests, reporters with cameras, and dozens of activists, many holding signs. The campaigners were there not so much to protest. Most wanted press coverage because the gala was known as the premier event of the year. Reporters often interviewed the activists, which brought attention to their myriad causes.

It was a motley crew. In other words, there seemed to be a placard for every conceivable special interest: Some signs were inscribed with "Support Israel," "America Wanted for the Murder of Muslims," or "U.S. Aid for Ghana." Others focused on more local matters, such as "School Choice Now," "Keep Abortion Legal," or "Vote Sampson for Congress."

Trudy, a woman passing out "Peace in the Middle East" leaflets, was not present to garner attention from journalists. She was peeved about being excluded from the guest list and wanted an explanation. She confronted Roger, who was navigating the front walkway.

"Hey, Roger, why weren't we invited?"

"You know why. Because your cause is political. You're not a 501(c)(3). It's policy."

"So, you're against peace?'

"Come on, Trudy. Everyone's in favor of peace. It's nice to see you again." Roger pushed his way through the crowd and into the hotel.

The lobby was ultramodern with a Picassoesque statue; a foot protruded from the brain. Roger interpreted it as a metaphorical kick in the head. There were also variations of amoeba-shaped furniture, a chandelier that appeared to have been borrowed from the *Star Wars* film set, futuristic chairs shaped like coconut halves, and a sign that read "Baltimore Charity Gala – 4th Floor."

Security guards hustled two activists, trying to sneak into the elevator, out of the building. They wore T-shirts, printed with the name of their cause: "The Anti-Terrorism Brigade."

The ballroom on the fourth floor was dressed to the nines, as were the guests. It had ethereal mint-colored drapery, a green-and-gold floral rug, circular tables covered with white tablecloths, and lush flowers on virtually every surface. A stage with a wooden podium was at one end of the room, adjacent to a string quartet. The instrumentalists were ready to begin their show, but not yet playing for the crowd.

Roger approached the podium and spoke into the microphone. He looked over the sea of faces; every table seemed to be occupied. Guests were enjoying their dinner; each had been served a chicken leg, a cut of steak, a salad, and a garlic dinner roll.

"I'm Roger Adams of Environmental Action. Welcome to our annual gathering. All charities in the area were invited, and I'm happy to report that everyone sent at least one representative. Tonight will be an opportunity to find ways to work together, to raise money, to boost awareness, to create bridges. In other words, I expect to see a lot of schmoozing."

There was laughter from the crowd.

"First, let me introduce some of the nonprofit directors."

Roger pulled a piece of paper from his pocket and spoke into the mic. "Carl Fox of the Cancer Survivor League."

Carl stood to applause and raised his arms like a boxing champ. He was a seventy-two-year-old hulk of a man who had retired from a career in the Marine Corps. He liked to tell people he was "crazy like a fox" in that he was game for just about anything. He was daring and spontaneous, although his detractors would have described him as a conspiracy theorist who suffered from a tendency to exaggerate his exploits.

Roger announced, "Dr. Kara Carson of the Middle East Poverty Foundation for Women and Girls."

Kara stood to applause and flirtatiously raised her wineglass to Roger as if making a toast.

Roger glanced at his notes and read the next name. "Ellen Garcia of the Hungry Child Network."

Ellen rose and sent air kisses to the crowd. Her hair was uninhibited; it represented the cauldron of untamed thoughts that pulsed under her seemingly mild demeanor. She was Native American by birth, sixty-two years old, and a devotee of karma, reincarnation, and Buddhism. She had taught classes on past-life regression in her younger days but had decided later in life that feeding underprivileged children was a better use of her time.

"Dr. Bill Seeks of LGBTQ Rights." Roger's eyes scanned the crowd until he found Bill's winsome smile.

Bill stood to applause.

Roger continued in the same vein until he had called out all the names, and then he stepped off the platform and headed toward his table. But there was an unexpected and unfortunate interruption.

Four activists with signage—including Anna Green (the leader of the group) and her sidekick, Joy—had sneaked past security. They carried placards that read "Animals are people, too," "Over 100 billion animals were killed for food this year," and "Meat on your plate. Blood on your hands."

The activists stormed into the ballroom, chanting and shouting as if the building was on fire.

"Steak, flesh, legs, tits. We smell the blood of some hypocrites."

There was a low hum of conversation by rattled attendees. The activists repeated their chants while periodically shouting "Shame on you" at individual invitees.

Two guests, Lila and Terri, seemed particularly irritated by the disruption. Lila yelled, "It's the loony animal rights activists. They crashed last year. And the year before."

Terri put down her chicken leg and stood. "Don't they realize no one cares? They're so damn evil."

Uniformed guards marched toward the protestors.

Terri tossed her napkin on the table and confronted Joy. "Animals are not people, honey. How dare you put them on the same level!"

"You're an arrogant human. You should be ashamed."

Terri grabbed Joy's sign, and the two tussled, knocking over a chair and forcing guests to abandon their seats. The guards tried to break up the fight while Anna approached Roger.

"Hello, Roger."

"Hi, Anna."

"You're looking awfully hypocritical tonight. You outdid yourself with so many plates of dead animals. Let's see. I saw dead cows, dead hens. My goodness, there must be at least five hundred."

"Look, it's nothing against you or your cause. It's just that your mission doesn't fit with ours. This event's about charities working together. No one can support animal rights without losing donors."

"Donors? Really? Is that your excuse?"

"People don't want to stop eating meat, Anna. They don't want to change their lifestyle."

"They just like to point their finger at the evil corporations. Right?"

Roger hesitated, then laughed. "Yeah. That pretty much sums it up."

"But you're an environmentalist. Even if you don't care about the suffering of animals, you're supposed to care about climate change. Meat-eating is a major cause."

Roger stared at her, speechless.

Anna continued, "Consistency can be a real drag, huh?"

"Okay. Okay," Roger said. "I'm a hypocrite. But we need donations to stay afloat. We're able to do some good things with that money."

"Why don't you come by my place next week? You can meet the family—my parents, my grandmother. It's a multi-generational house. Let's find a way to work together." Anna handed him a business card as the guards steered her and the other activists out of the conference room.

Roger walked alongside the group, figuring it was his job as host to ensure their rapid removal.

As the guards shoved the activists into the elevator, Roger smiled at Anna and waved. "See you next year."

Anna glared at him as the elevator doors shut.

Roger dumped Anna's business card into a nearby trash can and rejoined the gala.

❧

Things were wrapping up. Guests had finished their meals, and servers were clearing dirty plates. The quartet played, and some people danced, but most folks had already left or were making their departure.

Kara rummaged through her purse, found the tiny container

of pheromone perfume, and dabbed some on her neck. Then she strolled over to Roger.

"Are you the infamous Roger Adams?"

Roger smiled. "I could be."

"Well, you're looking quite distinguished in your crimson tie."

"And you, mademoiselle, with your ruby red scarf."

"Are you still married?"

"Why do you always ask me that, Kara?"

"What can I say? I'm a repetitive person."

"Yes, I'm still married. Sorry to report the bad news."

"It's not bad news. Who says it's bad news? I'm just curious. I ask everyone." Kara stopped Ellen, who was heading toward the elevator. "Excuse me, ma'am. Are you married?"

Ellen looked at Kara like she had three heads.

Then Kara shouted at an elderly gentleman across the room. "Sir. Sir. What about you? Are you married?"

The man did not hear and moved out of sight.

Kara looked at Roger. "That man's always so mysterious. I think he's a spy."

Roger laughed. "How can an attractive woman like you be single?"

"I have to fend them off every day. Frankly, it's a full-time job. I barely have time to dance with my dog," Kara joked.

Roger chuckled. "You have a dog?"

"No. I lied." Kara grinned.

"I think you're the mysterious one." Roger smiled.

Ellen stepped into the elevator next to Carl, who was showing off his flashy pedometer watch while marching in place.

Carl bragged, "Eleven thousand steps, and it's not even eleven."

She replied, "Good for you, Carl." She turned to Roger,

who was standing nearby, and shouted, "Hey, Roger, want me to hold the door?"

"Sure, Ellen." Roger scurried into the elevator.

Kara slipped in behind him, making the lift crowded with eight people.

There were fifty floors per the display; they were on the fourth floor. The doors closed.

Carl said to Kara, "I like your cologne, Dr. Carson. It makes me want to take you to the woodshed for a quick paddle and a spicy eggplant." He gave her a suggestive wink. "Lucky for you, I'm gay. Crazy Carl's been gay for 8,674 days."

"I thought sexual orientation was related to biological factors that begin before birth," Kara said.

"Maybe for most people. Not me. It's been 8,674 days."

In the elevator was Bernie Cruz, a twenty-five-year-old Mexican American. He was a former honor student and worked as a sales associate at an auto parts store, even though he looked like a member of a Harley-Davidson motorcycle gang with his tattoos, black leather jacket, and ponytail.

Standing beside Bernie were rich kids Angus Van Graff and his adopted brother, Keiko. Keiko was half Asian and half white. He was the child of a former Van Graff housekeeper who was deported back to her home country of Japan. Unlike his mother, Keiko was "legal." This was due to a Supreme Court decision which ruled that children born on U.S. soil were citizens even when they were the offspring of immigrants who had sneaked into the country. The Van Graffs had agreed to raise the boy and had, in fact, legally adopted him.

Keiko was twenty-three and looked up to his twenty-five-year-old brother, Angus, who was possibly the biggest jerk in Baltimore.

Angus had no appreciation for hard work and hated poor people. He had an entitled attitude and relished fast cars, junk food, wild parties, and sleazy women, whom he described as "Kmart tarts." He often said, "I'm gonna fetch me a Kmart tart."

Despite Keiko's humble beginnings and "low-class genes" (as Angus liked to say), the older brother accepted his younger sibling as a genuine member of the family. This was largely because Keiko did everything his brother asked; Angus enjoyed being what he called "the proud owner of a manservant."

The final person in the elevator was Bailey Iverson, a nineteen-year-old single mom. She was uneducated, was broke, and did not know what she wanted from life. She muddled through each day, hoping things would eventually fall into place. She felt as if there were a funnel of rain above her head. She had heard about this phenomenon on the news. Weather experts called it a "precipitation shaft." Bailey believed that she—and only she—faced obstacles and cloudbursts while everyone else was granted eternal sunshine. She volunteered, sporadically, at a food bank; it was a way for her to get first dibs on the free food. She had been gifted a ticket to the gala because no one else at the charity wanted to attend.

Bernie pushed the knob for "lobby," but the elevator moved up.

Angus berated Bernie. "It's going up, Poncho. You pushed the wrong button."

Roger said, "He pushed the right button, and you don't need to talk to him like that."

Angus shrugged and let out an exasperated sigh.

"You can talk to him any way you want," Keiko, the always-loyal minion, whispered to his brother, who puffed up like a peacock.

Bernie stared at Angus and spoke firmly. "My *name* is Bernie."

"Got it, Poncho," Angus teased.

Bernie rolled his eyes.

Roger pressed "lobby," but the lift did not change direction.

"Let me do it." Angus shoved Roger to the side and placed his thumb firmly on the "lobby" knob for a full five seconds, but the elevator continued upward. Then he pushed floor after floor to no avail.

Bailey stood in the corner, pretending to be invisible.

"You think that damn thing's broken?" Carl asked.

Angus pointed at Carl. "Folks, we have a brain surgeon on board."

"I knew I should have taken the stairs," Ellen said.

"It's no big deal," Kara responded. "We'll go up. Then we'll come back down."

Keiko whispered to Angus, "We're gonna be late for the party."

Angus once again pushed several buttons, but the elevator continued upward, past the twentieth floor.

Then things got wacky. There were deafening and sustained squeals; the elevator sounded like it was in severe pain. Ellen and Bailey placed their hands over their ears. The noise eventually subsided.

"Anyone got any WD-40?" Roger tried to lighten the mood.

"I've got some Prozac." Kara laughed.

Roger picked up the elevator phone. "It's not working."

Angus said, "Let me try." It was dead, so he pushed the disconnect lever repeatedly to no avail.

Everyone took out their cell phones.

"No service," Kara said.

"Me neither," Ellen replied.

"Can anyone get a signal?" Kara asked.

Everyone shook their heads.

As the lift passed the thirtieth floor, the elevator came to an abrupt stop. Then it jerked, moved upward a little, sputtered, made a wheezing sound, and squealed again. It repeated this procedure of stop, jerk, move, sputter, wheeze, and squeal over and over. It seemed to be limping toward death.

Everyone, except Carl, gasped or screamed in unison with each stomach-turning jolt.

Carl seemed to be enjoying the adventure. He pretended to be slalom skiing. "It's hopping and popping. Reminds me of the time I was in a Jeep Wrangler speeding through North Korea with the People's Army on my tail. They called me the Jeep Jockey back then."

Everyone stared at Carl like he was crazy.

Then there was a gigantic jolt, stronger than the previous ones. Bailey and Bernie fell to the ground while the others clung to the walls.

"It's gonna crash. We're gonna die!" Ellen was hysterical.

Bernie yelled, "Someone out there help us!"

Kara tried to calm everyone down. "Hey, it's not gonna crash."

"Thanks for the prediction, Einstein. Makes me feel a whole lot better," Angus said.

"Elevators are held by steel cables and counterweights," Kara added. "Only one elevator in the U.S. has ever fallen. It was in the 1940s, and it was because a plane crashed into the building."

"How do you know this?" Roger looked impressed.

"I know lots of useless facts."

"Can I have some of your Prozac?" Ellen said to Kara.

Roger pushed button after button, but the elevator continued past the forty-fifth floor, sputtering and squealing.

Bailey spoke for the first time. "Do you think this elevator's haunted?"

"I hope it's not Frederico, my dead ex-husband," Ellen replied. "He said he'd come back and get me."

The elevator reached the top floor: the fiftieth. And it halted altogether. It was eerily silent; it seemed dead.

"Why'd it stop?" Bernie asked.

"It seems to have a mind of its own," Ellen said. "Maybe it's lost its urge to frighten the bejesus out of us."

"I think it's jammed." Roger again pushed button after button. The doors would not open.

"Maybe it blew a fuse," Kara speculated.

"We could be trapped in here for hours or fucking days." Angus banged his fist against the wall.

Suddenly, things got a whole lot worse. Everyone went blind.

"Oh my God. I can't see." Kara panicked.

"Me neither," Roger said.

Bailey rubbed her eyes. "Oh no."

Bernie yelled, "What's going on?

Ellen fell to the ground. "I'm blind. I'm completely blind."

"Shit. What the hell's happening?" Angus sounded genuinely afraid for the first time.

"Angus. Help… Help me," Keiko stuttered.

Everyone had their arms out, feeling for the walls and each other, except for Carl, who chuckled and spoke in a singsong way, "Marco Polo."

"Maybe it's just dark," Bailey offered.

"I don't think so." Kara could no longer calm her fellow passengers because she was in full-fledged panic mode.

Everyone, except Carl, was frightened; they cried, moaned, screamed, prayed, whimpered, or ranted. Angus folded himself into a ball on the ground and wept uncontrollably, proving that when no one was watching he was more like a marshmallow than the tough guy he purported to be.

"This is really, really bad," Kara confessed. "I think you're right, Ellen. I think we're gonna die."

Chapter Two

PAST TENSE, FUTURE IMPERFECT

They were closer to heaven, but it felt like hell. The eight gala guests were stranded in the elevator on the top floor of the Zelles Hotel, and they had been blind for a full five minutes—a long time to feel helpless, frozen in fear, and believe the end was imminent. An avalanche of thoughts tumbled through Kara's mind. Would she starve to death? Would there be another unexpected catastrophe? Perhaps the elevator walls would move inward, squeezing her into bloody mush, or the ceiling would descend, pounding her into a fleshy stump. Maybe swords would protrude from the walls and eviscerate her. Perhaps the floor would collapse, and she would plummet to a fiery and gruesome end.

Kara wondered how everyone had gone blind

at the same time. Had gas been injected into the lift? If so, by whom? Could it have been methanol, which can destroy the optic nerve? Perhaps there had been poison in the food at the event. Or maybe an all-powerful, evil entity was getting revenge on those with a good heart, on those who did charity work. At this point, anything seemed possible, no matter how outrageous.

Kara also reminisced about her life. She reflected on the irony of dying next to one of the men on her "marriage bucket list." She pondered over her self-absorbed mother, who had always been concerned with appearances and who did not have a philanthropic bone in her nipped-and-tucked body. She wondered if anyone would ever invent a functioning phero-mone perfume and who would head up her nonprofit after her demise. Kara contemplated many things while collapsed on the floor with her hands over her face, wrapped in the depths of doom and sorrow.

But suddenly and without explanation, things got better.

"I can see again." Kara popped up, elated.

"Me too!" Ellen shouted. "What about you guys?"

"My peepers are fully operational." Carl did a little jig.

"Yeah," Roger said.

Everyone nodded or replied affirmatively, expressing relief and confusion about what had transpired. Their eyesight had been inexplicably restored. It was as if a magic wand had been waved or a fairy godmother had miraculously appeared. Perhaps God, Allah, Brahma, Buddha, or some other omni-scient power had fought off the evil entity and come to their aid. Kara did not care what the truth was. She was relieved.

"This whole thing is really weird," Bailey said.

"Do you think we're dead?" Kara asked.

"No way," Keiko replied.

Roger tinkered with his cell. "My phone's blank, and it was fully charged when I got on the elevator."

Everyone reexamined their phones and found theirs were not working either.

"It's not just lacking a signal. It's kaput. Nothing," Bernie added. "And mine was charged, too."

Kara glanced at the elevator's indicator panel, baffled. "How are we on the fifty-first floor? This floor doesn't exist. There are only fifty floors in this building."

Everyone gazed at the digital display, bewildered by the well-lit "51."

"I think you're right, Kara," Ellen said. "I think we're dead."

"This reminds me of the time I drove 4,200 miles between Los Angeles and Las Vegas." Carl chuckled. "Turned out my odometer was broken."

"I can't believe I'm saying this, but maybe Crazy Carl is right," Ellen said. "Maybe the gauge is broken. Maybe we're really on the fiftieth floor."

"Good try, Ellen, but I don't buy it," Roger said.

"Me neither. There wouldn't be a 51 in a fifty-story building," Kara reasoned. "It isn't logical. You don't invent something just for the heck of it."

Angus looked up toward the heavens. "I promise I'll give all my money to charity if we get back to the first floor."

"You mean Dad's money," Keiko interjected.

Suddenly, the elevator started moving downward.

Angus said in disbelief, "Wow, it fucking worked."

"Thank you, Frederico," Ellen spoke into the ether, as if she believed her dead ex-husband was the mischief maker behind the freakish events.

The elevator did not stop at any of the floors on its way down even though all the buttons were pushed.

The eight were silent, transfixed on the digital display as

the lift moved past 35, then past 30, and then past 25. They seemed to think any sound would jinx the situation.

When the lift reached the tenth floor, Angus blurted out, "I'm totally gonna give a hundred dollars to charity."

The eight continued to eye the display, praying the lift would stay on track.

The elevator reached the ground floor, but the doors remained closed. Roger pushed the "lobby" and "open doors" buttons, again and again. Nothing happened.

Suddenly, another bizarre thing occurred: A message appeared on the digital display. It read "Be back here on July 4 at 10 pm. Don't be early."

"Be back in two weeks?" Roger said.

"Maybe it's a practical joke," Bailey offered.

"Who's doing this to us?" Bernie screamed. "Let us out, whoever you are."

Angus tried to pry the doors open; Keiko and Roger joined the effort. Their attempt failed.

"Whoever this is…" Kara said calmly. "If you can hear me, we promise we'll be back on the fourth."

With that, the doors slid open, and everyone dashed out, relieved.

✤

The Picasso-like statue was missing, and Roger mumbled, "Hey, that kick in the head's gone." There was a large gold sculpture of Queen Victoria in its place.

The lobby was radically different. The furnishings were no longer modern; they appeared to be from the Victorian era. There was a nineteenth-century sofa, walnut parlor tables, B & H oil lamps, a wooden slant-top secretary, and a framed vintage advertisement for the play *A Doll's House*. In addition to the period furnishings, yellow "Under Construction" signs were scattered about, and a placard above the elevator read "Out of Order."

Kara figured this was just another screwy development in an evening that had involved so many screwy developments. The past hour or so had, in effect, defied gravity and defied logic. This new reality seemed to be anything but real. Kara felt as if she had been sucked into a vacuum and was flailing about, trying to get her bearings, trying to survive.

She and the other seven wandered out of the hotel entrance. It was no better outside.

"What the hell's going on?" Angus shouted as he scanned the sidewalk, street, and nearby buildings.

It appeared to be a mixture of past eras, a mishmash of time periods ranging from the 1700s to the 1970s. Several vehicles littered the street, from a Model T Ford to a street car, a Plymouth Suburban station wagon, and a horseless prairie schooner. There were old-fashioned lampposts and a phone booth. "Under Construction" signs and yellow do-not-enter barricade tape were positioned to caution folks away from the Zelles Hotel.

Roger checked his cell. "It's still dead."

There was a chorus of "me toos" and assorted complaints by the others about their nonworking phones.

"Maybe we're in a parallel universe or a time loop," Kara speculated.

"You mean like *Groundhog Day*?" Keiko asked.

"But nothing's repeated," Bernie said.

"I saw a movie about a time loop once," Bailey mumbled. "*Happy Death Day*."

"Some experts don't think time is linear," Kara added. "Even the ancient Incas and Mayans thought it was cyclical and quantic."

"This looks like the past," Roger said. "But how could we be in the past? There's no such thing as time travel."

"Seems more like *Back to the Future* or *Planet of the Apes* than *Groundhog Day*," Keiko added. "Wouldn't it be cool if this place were controlled by monkeys?"

"I want to go back. I don't want to be here anymore." Bailey ran to the hotel entrance and pulled on the now-locked doors in a frenzy. "Let me in. Let me in."

Kara placed her arm around Bailey. "It's okay. We'll figure this out. They're probably gonna take us back on July fourth. It'll be our independence day. It's only two weeks away."

"We're all exhausted," Roger said. "Let's go home and regroup in the morning. You want to meet here at eleven? Then we can go to the police station and find out what the hell's going on."

"Sounds like a plan, boss," Carl replied.

Bailey moved away from the hotel entrance. "What if my apartment isn't there?"

Roger pointed at the station wagon. "This car is from the 1970s, so we can't be farther back in time than that. If your apartment's not there, maybe you have friends or relatives who were alive in the 1970s?"

Everyone again nodded.

"In the movie *Yesterday*, only a few things had changed. Everything else was the same, so maybe our houses and families are waiting for us," Keiko said optimistically.

"But what if they aren't?" Bailey asked.

"Then get a hotel," Roger replied.

Carl executed a military salute while the others nodded, indicating they were amenable to the plan.

Angus and Keiko departed together. Bailey, Carl, and Ellen hit the subway station.

Kara turned to Roger. "Can I go with you? Considering everything that's happened, I don't really want to be alone."

"Sure. My wife can fix up the spare room for you."

"Can I come, too?" Bernie asked. "I'm new to Baltimore."

"Sure, Bernie."

Roger, Kara, and Bernie made their way through the streets, dumbfounded by the disjointed surroundings. Every step, every turn, was an unexpected surprise. It was like wandering around a well-resourced prop room at a movie studio.

The threesome saw three-wheeler bikes from 1885, a USPS mail collection box from the 1960s, and a pair of 1920 Ball-Band high-top sneakers on the pavement. There were storefront mannequins circa 1900, outfitted with bell-shaped skirts, cinched waistlines, modest turtleneck blouses, and gigantic flower hats. There were billboards in the style of the 1930s, advertising Coca-Cola, Stouffer's frozen foods, Delta Airlines, and Comet cleaning powder.

They arrived at Roger's house, which had undergone substantial changes—as had the neighbor's house where the sewer leak had been. Roger's formerly high-tech abode was now low-tech with a second story. It was painted cream instead of the original light brown. There were also two birch trees in the front yard; there had been no trees that morning, only hydrangea and lilies.

"Are you sure it says 822?" Roger asked.

Bernie checked the house number again. "Yep."

Roger rang the bell; an elderly man poked his head out.

"Is… is Joan here?" Roger asked.

"Do you realize it's almost midnight?" the man barked.

"I apologize."

"You got the wrong house. Nobody by that name." The man closed the door.

Kara's condo complex was the next stop. It was no longer

bumblebee yellow; it was painted gray. Other than the paint job, it looked the same as earlier in the day.

Roger checked the directory. "There's no Kara Carson. What's your unit number?"

"302," Kara replied.

"There's no 302."

"Let's try 304." Kara pushed the buzzer.

No answer.

She pushed it, again and again.

Finally, a voice responded through the intercom system. "Yeah?"

"I'm looking for 302. Kara Carson," she said.

"There is no 302. And you shouldn't be waking people up. Don't you realize there's a curfew? You're gonna get thrown in jail if the cops catch you."

"Sorry. It's an emergency. I need to get in touch with the person in 302."

"There hasn't been a 302 for 40 years."

"Thank you." Kara mumbled under her breath, "Forty years?"

Nothing made sense, but the threesome moved on to Bernie's place. He had been renting a room in an old Tudor-style dwelling. As they trudged along the empty streets, the neighborhood began to lend itself to a *Leave it to Beaver* vibe.

Bernie stopped short in front of a vacant lot, wide-mouthed. "It was here. I was renting a room in a house right here. I know it was built before 1970."

Two homeless men with an encampment behind a block wall were on the lot. One wore a checkered bathrobe over ordinary pants; the other was outfitted in gray coveralls. Mr. Coveralls came forward. Bizarre data floated in the air in front of his chest: CQ = 75.8.

The threesome approached the man.

"What's that on your chest?" Kara inquired, referring to the CQ and number.

The man glanced down to see stains on his clothes. "It's called mud, lady. I don't got no washer." He looked at her designer evening wear. "I'm not fancy folks like you. So why don't you beat it?"

"I'm sorry. I didn't mean to offend you," Kara said.

The man appeared livid and moved back behind the wall.

The guy in the bathrobe walked toward them. The equation "CQ = 71.9" was in front of his chest.

Bernie spoke to him. "Excuse me, sir. We're victims of time travel. We're from the future. Can you tell us what year it is?"

The man ranted and thrashed his arms about; he seemed like an escapee from a nuthouse. "Time travel? Don't tell anyone. They'll take you to their secret camp and kill you. God will never find you. You're one of the chosen…"

Kara, Roger, and Bernie were alarmed by the man's erratic behavior, so they scrambled away.

They could hear him screaming in the distance, "Don't tell anyone. The future's not welcome here. Run. Hurry. Don't let them catch you."

When the man was out of sight, the threesome slowed to a walk.

"That was strange," Kara remarked. "Do you think there's any truth in what he was saying?"

"I think he's mentally ill," Roger replied. "But, those numbers. What are they?"

"Maybe we're the only ones who can see them," Kara hypothesized.

"What could CQ mean? It can't be 'Cute Quality' cause those dudes definitely weren't cute," Bernie said.

"True." Roger laughed. "Cute is not their strong point."

"C could stand for… cuddly, criminal, clever, creepy," Bernie added. "Creepy fits those guys pretty well."

"CQ is normally an abbreviation for the culture quotient," Kara said, once again proving she was a walking search engine. "It's similar to IQ or the intelligence quotient. It relates to cultural awareness and sensitivity. It's normally used by businesses or institutions to evaluate how well employees harmonize with a diverse workplace."

"It can't be that," Roger argued. "Otherwise, those guys would have much lower scores. They're clearly outliers."

"They'd be in the single digits for sure," Bernie added.

The threesome moved to a final stop: Kara's mother's house. It was brick with white trim and a fireplace. It looked pretty much the same as it did before the elevator incident, but there was an old Volkswagen bug in the driveway.

"My mom has a navy Mercedes. I don't think she ever had a Volkswagen. Plus, I'm not even sure if she was living here in the seventies. She might have bought the house in the eighties."

Kara went to the front door and rang the bell. There was no answer, so she peered through the window.

"This isn't my mom's furniture. She wouldn't be caught dead with an orange polka-dot couch." Kara turned to Roger. "What about your parents?"

"They weren't in Baltimore in the 1970s."

"Guys, you said this was the last place." Bernie was starting to limp. "I'm zonked."

The threesome noticed a run-down motel in the distance with a banner that read "Fresh Aire Motel." They headed toward it.

After a long and exhausting hike, Angus and Keiko arrived at the grand estate they'd called home since birth. It was on the ritzy side of Baltimore and looked much the same as it had that morning. It was a gorgeous stone structure, partially covered in ivy.

Angus rang the bell, and a butler opened the door. The equation "CQ = 29.9" floated in front of his chest.

"Is this the Van Graff residence?" Angus asked.

"No. That was a previous occupant. They haven't lived here for almost a century."

"A century?" Angus was taken aback. "Where are they?"

"I wouldn't know, sir. Rumor has it that they left the state after filing bankruptcy."

"Bankruptcy?" Angus exclaimed.

"There was something about embezzlement and a prison sentence. Some say the family moved to Rome, Georgia. Are you related to them?"

The boys shook their heads violently.

"Is there anything else I can do for you?" the butler asked.

The boys shook their heads again, and the butler started to close the door.

"Wait. What does that say?" Keiko pointed at the CQ equation hovering in the air.

The butler looked down and saw the words "Pierre Cardin Paris" on the handkerchief poking out of his pocket.

"It's a Pierre Cardin. Have a nice evening, boys."

The butler closed the door.

Keiko jogged through the expansive side yard of the residence. Angus tagged along.

"What's a goddamn CQ?" Angus asked.

"Who knows? Do you think that man was right about Mom and Dad?"

"No. He's a fucking idiot. He doesn't know shit."

"A century ago? It doesn't make sense." Keiko climbed the redwood rungs that led to a tree house.

Angus followed.

"Why are we going to the fort?" Angus pointed at a broken piece of redwood. "Hey, dickhead. That board's still cracked. I remember when you fell and broke your leg. I laughed for a fucking week."

The tree house rested between two thick branches. It had openings for windows and a door.

The boys crawled into the fort.

"It looks the same." Angus noticed his initials were still carved into the floor.

Keiko folded his jacket into a pillow, lay down, and tried to go to sleep.

"You're kidding?" Angus exclaimed. "This is bullshit. Why aren't we going to a hotel?"

❧

Ellen, Carl, and Bailey had been all over town, attempting to locate someone they knew—anyone at all. They came up dry. They ran into a passerby during the early part of their journey. She was hurrying home while trying not to be noticed and had alerted them to the curfew and the heavy-handed police who were patrolling the streets in search of scofflaws. The passerby had the equation "CQ = 61.8" hovering in front of her chest. When Ellen asked about it, the woman became uneasy and quickly dashed away.

Due to the curfew warning, the trio jumped behind trees, ducked next to parked cars, and scurried into dark alleys when vehicles approached. They took care not to be seen by cops or anyone else for that matter. Now they stood outside a luxury hotel, counting their cash. They only had sixty dollars, all combined.

"We can't afford this place," Ellen said. "And there's no way our credit cards will work."

"This situation reminds me of the time—" Carl started.

"Not now, Carl," Ellen interrupted him.

"Yes, ma'am." Carl chuckled and used his fingers to mimic a zipping of the lips.

"Come with me. I'm good at this sort of thing," Bailey instructed. "And don't make eye contact with the lady at the front desk."

The female hotel clerk was chatting with a guest, and no one else was in the lobby.

Bailey confidently strolled through the entrance, past the reception desk, and down a hallway; Ellen and Carl followed closely behind.

The trio entered the corporate wing of the establishment, adjacent to the pool. Bailey grabbed two lounge chair towels from a shelf. Carl and Ellen did the same.

"You're pretty resourceful, young lady." Carl smiled.

Bailey led them into a conference room where the tables were covered with freshly ironed white linens that grazed the rug. Bailey crawled under a table.

Ellen raised the tablecloth to see that Bailey had made a pillow out of one towel and draped the other over her body like a blanket.

"They never come in the conference rooms at night," Bailey said.

"I'm too old for this," Ellen complained.

Then she and Carl got on their hands and knees. They joined Bailey under the table.

⤚

Kara entered the Fresh Aire Motel while Roger and Bernie hid in the parking lot. The lobby had cheap wall paneling, a tile floor, and a no-frills wooden counter. There was a dial-up phone on the desk, a clock, and a display case for brochures, which included information about rental cars and attractions in the area.

The clerk at the front desk was a rather odd-looking chap. He was dressed in sixteenth-century short breeches, a padded gold and purple waistcoat, stockings, a codpiece, a floppy purple hat, and a curly wig. There was a narrow ruff around his neck, which was essentially an accordion-like collar. The equation "CQ = 81.8" floated in front of his chest.

Behind the counter were old-fashioned key cubbies and a sign that read "$70 for 1 guest. $85 for 2 guests."

Kara was guarded. She wanted to be careful about what she said due to the warning from the guy in the bathrobe. She was unsure whether he was a lunatic or telling the truth about being hauled off to secret camps and killed.

"How many?" The clerk was all business.

"Just one." Kara smiled. "Just me. One night." She glanced at his chest. "What's a CQ?"

"No idea. I need to see your I.D."

Kara handed over her driver's license, and he examined it.

He shot daggers at Kara, which alarmed her.

But then he roared with laughter.

"Boy, the Motor Vehicle Administration is so screwed up. Never trust those government types."

"What do you mean?" Kara muttered, trying to tread lightly.

The clerk pointed at the date on the driver's license. "It says it expires in 2025."

"Yeah?" she whispered.

"That's a hundred years ago. It's 2125." He stared at her suspiciously, as if she was either an idiot or a criminal with a fake I.D.

Kara let out a laugh. "Ah, that's right. 2125.... Those government types."

"Cash or credit?"

Kara handed him a credit card, and he ran it through a machine.

He once again stared at her like she was a crook. "Declined."

"Sorry." Kara placed cash on the counter.

The clerk examined the money. "Are you sure you want to use this?"

"Why wouldn't I?"

"These are rare bills, Mrs. Carson. They're worth more than face value."

"Yes. I want to use them."

Kara was given a key, left the lobby, and motioned Roger and Bernie, who were still hiding in the parking lot, to join her. She opened the door to the room, and the threesome went inside.

"You're not going to believe this," Kara exclaimed. "It's one hundred years in the future. It's 2125."

Chapter Three

LUDDITE LAND

It was June 2025, the morning after the nonprofit gala. A massive crowd of reporters and onlookers stood near a flagpole and a tree outside the Baltimore Police Department. The building was white with brickwork and six columns in the front.

A podium had been installed next to a set of steps; it held various microphones belonging to the media. Reporters from channels WBAL, WBFF, WJZ, and WMDT were in attendance, as were journalists from the *Baltimore Sun* and the *Capital Gazette*.

The police chief and a contingent of uniformed officers paraded out of the building. The chief took his position at the podium while the other officers stood behind him for moral support.

"Eight individuals—five males and three females—did not return from last night's charity event." The chief addressed the crowd. "We have tracked their cell phones, and the signals end on the top floor of the Zelles Hotel. We are investigating

every room in the building. We're also requesting that the public send us any information they have."

A journalist shouted, "What about the other disappearances?"

"Yes, there are reports of disappearances from other elevators, many outside Baltimore. We are in touch with law enforcement in those jurisdictions."

The journalist continued, "Can you tell us the names of the people who disappeared?"

"Not at this time. Their families have not yet been contacted. We're not taking any more questions. Thank you."

There was chatter from the crowd as the chief and his fellow officers marched back into the police station.

&

It was morning in 2125. Kara, Roger, and Bernie left the motel and headed for the library, hoping to get some clarity on their strange situation.

"Too bad there wasn't a TV in the room," Kara said.

"For seventy bucks, we're lucky there was a bed," Roger quipped.

Kara laughed; she always laughed at his jokes.

During the walk, the threesome observed an AAA Staging Company truck parked at a residential listing. There was a broker's sign in the yard, and a rider noted that the place would be open from four p.m. to eight p.m.

"Wow, that company's still in business," Roger mumbled.

They arrived at the library, which appeared normal. There were rows of books, tables with chairs, a reading room, and two staff members at the circulation desk. The place had no patrons, except for a man and a boy in the children's section.

Kara and Bernie went to the stacks and flipped through books.

Roger approached a librarian with a CQ of 48.9. She was wearing a 1980s-style dress.

"Where are the computers?" Roger asked.

The librarian flashed a bewildered look. "Computers?"

Roger adjusted his request. "Old newspapers."

"Microfiche." She pointed.

"By the way, what does CQ mean?"

"Never heard of it, but you can check the card catalog."

Roger searched the card catalog but could not find anything related to "CQ." Then he joined Bernie and Kara, who were scrolling through microfiche.

"Hey, look what I found." Kara motioned to a newspaper column from 2026 that read "Still no sign of Baltimore's Charity Eight, who vanished a year ago."

Roger and Bernie glanced over her shoulder.

"Cool," Bernie said. "They're talking about us."

The piece included photos of the eight.

Kara grimaced. "It looks like I'm bald and ate a roasted blimp. My mother wanted to embarrass me. As usual."

Roger stumbled upon an article titled "Study: 85% of Americans Prefer Stairs over Elevators." He read the piece aloud to Kara and Bernie. "Are elevators cosmic wormholes, the manifestation of the fourth dimension, or portals for alien abduction? A majority of Americans support the decision by the White House to hire paranormal experts to investigate lifts throughout the nation."

"Tea-leaf readers to the rescue." Kara laughed.

"Here's another one." Roger focused on a different story. "Neo-luddites in high gear. Backlash against technology takes hold. Protestors around the world revolt against tech's invasion of privacy, the lack of well-made consumer products, hacking, and the loss of jobs to robots. Millions of people fight for privacy, simplicity, safety, product durability, and human dignity—embracing past eras in a moral rebellion."

Bernie pointed at a picture under the article; it portrayed people in clothing styles from various eras. "Seems like they dress to jibe with their favorite century."

"So that's why the motel clerk looked like a court jester." Kara grinned. "Hey, look at this. It's hilarious." She read the piece out loud. "The First World shows solidarity with the Third World by becoming the Third World itself. If you can't beat 'em, join 'em."

Roger laughed. "I bet the Flat Earth Society is raking in the bucks."

"True." Kara chuckled. "Unfortunately, its members have some awfully thin topsoil."

Roger came upon a photo depicting caged people at the zoo next to the headline "Local Zoo Profits Up (story on page 32)." Roger laughed. "At least *The Onion* is still around."

Kara and Bernie leaned over to see the picture.

"I love satire." Kara smiled.

"I bet that photo was staged for Instagram," Bernie added.

"This world's not totally backward," Kara joked. "People still waste time on moronic stunts so they can jack up their social media following."

Roger continued to scroll through articles.

"You guys hungry?" Kara stood. "There must be some food in this hinterland. Guess I'll be Henry the Navigator and go exploring."

"I'll come along." Bernie rose.

"See you later, Henry," Roger said. "Bring me back some unleavened bread or the heads of natives. Whatever you can find."

Kara and Bernie trotted off while Roger found a death notice for his wife.

The obituary read "Local Realtor dies in crash with semi-truck. Joan Adams of Adams Realty, age 54, died in a head-on collision. It has been a decade since her ex-husband, Roger, disappeared. Roger Adams was a well-known environmentalist and one of Baltimore's eight missing charity volunteers. Survivors include Joan's husband, Javier Gonzalez, and stepson, Josh Gonzalez."

The threesome left the library and sauntered down the sidewalk, munching on granola bars. Roger's mood was contemplative and somber.

"We're gonna go back, and you'll see your wife again." Kara tried to lift Roger's spirits. "You can make sure she doesn't get into that crash."

"What if her death was fate?" Roger asked.

"There must be a reason we're here," Kara replied. "What sort of evil overlord would time-travel us into Crazyville and then not let us go back and change the past? What would be the point?" Kara noticed an electronics store. "Let's go in. My phone's dead. I want to get a new one."

The store looked like a 1980s Radio Shack, but with more radios and less tech. There were old-fashioned record players, a jukebox, vintage phones, chords, electrical sockets, and LP record albums, among other consumer items.

As the threesome entered, Kara whispered to Roger, "I wonder if they have eight-track tapes. Nah. That's probably too advanced for them."

He laughed.

A clerk with a CQ of 52.8 stood behind a counter. His boss, who had a CQ of 88.9, sat at a desk, tallying numbers. There was a television perched high and anchored to the wall. It was airing the local news.

A TV journalist reported, "It will be sunny tomorrow with a two percent chance of rain."

Kara sashayed up to the counter and held out her smartphone. "I need to buy a cheap iPhone."

The clerk looked at her curiously. "An iPhone?"

"If you don't have it, a basic cell phone's fine."

Suddenly, the news shifted topics. Kara, Roger, Bernie, and the clerk gazed at the screen.

"Breaking news." The reporter appeared frazzled. "We are in the midst of an alien terrorist invasion. This is not a joke. These aliens, who look like you and me, are reportedly here to destroy society and take over the planet. They were apparently transported here by way of… well, elevators.

"Last night, three elevator people set fire to a store in Oregon, killing two employees. These terrorists were shot dead by police. This morning, two elevator people were arrested in South Carolina after they broke into fast-food billionaire Jack Farthing's estate with automatic rifles. There were no injuries or fatalities, but the elevator people were arrested and are likely to face the death penalty."

On the screen, there was footage of handcuffed elevator people being loaded into police vehicles.

The reporter continued, "And overseas, at least ninety-eight elevator people—or vates as they are called—have been captured and imprisoned: in South Korea, Russia, and Australia. Sixty-three vates were neutralized by law enforcement with help from the military."

The TV program aired additional footage of elevator people being arrested.

"Investigators are trying to determine if these terrorists are linked to the disappearances from elevators a century ago. There will be a curfew again tonight at ten p.m. Law enforcement will be searching the streets. Most elevator people have no place to stay, and they lack money. Be on the lookout for suspicious behavior, and be careful. Elevator people can be identified by their support of Big Tech, their use of antique currency, and their extremist ideas. If you see them, please alert the authorities. And do not approach them. Let me repeat: do not approach the vates. They are considered deadly."

During the news report, the electronics store clerk had inched over to his boss and mumbled in his ear.

Kara figured he was talking about her—the suspicious customer who had requested an iPhone—so she tried to rectify the situation.

"Excuse me, sir," she said to the clerk. "We just need a phone for a prop. We're putting on a play at the university."

"A prop?" the clerk replied.

"Yes. It obviously doesn't need to work. That would be absurd. A cell phone that works."

Kara roared with laughter.

"We don't have anything like that."

"Oh, okay," Kara said. "Thanks."

She whispered to Roger and Bernie, "Let's get out of here."

The threesome sprinted down the sidewalk until they were a reasonable distance from the store, then they slowed to a walk.

"Why would elevator people be violent?" Kara asked.

§

The threesome arrived at the Zelles to find Ellen, Carl, Angus, and Keiko waiting for them.

Bailey was in the distance pressing her forehead against the hotel's entry doors.

Kara talked a mile a minute. "They think we're terrorists and aliens. They're calling us 'elevator people.' Or 'vates' for short."

"What in heaven's name are you talking about?" Ellen looked confused.

"We have to hide our identity and fit in," Kara continued. "Otherwise, they'll arrest us, maybe even kill us."

"So, we aren't going to the police station?" Angus asked.

"No," Roger said. "They'd probably throw us in jail, and we'd miss our July fourth return date."

"Plus, there are people like us all over the world," Bernie added.

"They're others?" Carl said. "Well, I'll be damned. How many?"

"No idea," Roger replied.

Kara pointed at Bailey. "Is she okay?"

"Poor little chickadee," Carl replied. "She's despondent."

"Close to suicidal," Ellen added. "I tried to shake her out of it."

"How do you know all this shit?" Angus asked.

"We saw a news report…" Roger dove into the story while Kara went off to comfort Bailey.

The two women had a private conversation.

"Are you okay?" Kara asked.

"No," Bailey said.

"No?"

"No."

"We only have to tread water for two weeks. We're gonna make it back."

"You don't understand." Bailey wiped her tears.

"Don't understand what?"

"I have a little girl. Eva. She's only eleven months. She was with a babysitter. What's gonna happen to her?"

"What about Eva's dad?"

"He ditched me when I got pregnant."

"Do you have relatives?"

"Only my mom who hates me and refuses to meet Eva."

"I'm sure she'll take care of your daughter. Wait. What

am I saying? We'll go back, and it'll be the same night we left. Haven't you ever seen a movie about time travel? That's what always happens. The charity gala will end like normal, and you'll pick up Eva at the babysitter. It'll be like we were never here."

"You really think so?" Bailey rubbed her eyes.

"Yeah, I do. It's the only logical outcome. This time travel thing must be for us to learn some sort of lesson and take the information back to 2025. Come on, no more pouting."

Kara led Bailey back to the others.

"This place is creepy. It's fucking Luddite land." Angus picked up a soiled nineteenth-century top hat from the sidewalk with his fingertips and then dropped it as if it had cooties.

Roger asked, "Did anyone find friends or relatives, someone who could help us with food and shelter?"

Everyone shook their heads.

Roger stared at Angus and Keiko. "What about you two big shots? What about your family?"

"They moved to Rome," Angus said, omitting that it was Rome, Georgia.

"Must be nice dining on gourmet tortellini instead of running from the sixteenth century," Ellen quipped.

"It's dangerous to use our money, and the cops are sweeping the streets looking for vates," Roger said. "So, we're gonna need to get jobs."

"Jobs?" Angus and Keiko spoke in unison, horrified.

"Why were you two at a charity event anyway?" Kara asked. "You don't seem like the volunteer types."

"Dad said he wouldn't include us in the will unless we spent a year doing philanthropy," Keiko replied.

"We've made it through six months," Angus added. "It hasn't been that bad."

"That's downright admirable," Kara shot back. "We're so lucky to have our own two Mother Teresas."

Everyone laughed, except Angus and Keiko.

The group huddled and brainstormed on how to stay afloat for the next two weeks, pitching ideas on obtaining food and a place to stay. They could not remain on the street with curfews, and it would be impossible to evade the cops for so long. If they got thrown in jail, it could be a catastrophe. They might miss the all-important July fourth return date.

Their deliberation was interrupted by hunger pangs. Although Bailey, a resourceful and frugal gal, had led Ellen and Carl through the hotel halls that morning and helped them gather leftover food from guests' trays, they were still famished. After all, they had found only a few packages of crackers and a couple of uneaten rolls.

"I'm starving," Ellen said.

"I could eat a food truck," Carl added.

"Me too," Keiko joined in.

"I saw a church around the corner," Roger replied. "They give out free food to the homeless. Why don't we get some chow? We'll think better on a full stomach."

The Episcopal church was modest in size and sandwiched between two buildings. In front of it were abandoned shopping carts, trash cans, and a cluster of what appeared to be vagrants with CQ numbers ranging between 39 and 89. They mostly wore ragged and soiled clothes. The eight joined a line that winded through the front door.

When they got inside the church, they noticed food servers dishing out breakfast from behind banquet tables; these volunteers wore white caps and aprons. There were also refectory tables where the homeless ate. Some diners were standing and gabbing with their friends. Many eyed the eight suspiciously, partly due to their spiffy attire and partly because no one had ever seen these folks before.

Kara was baffled by what looked like a human toe on a chain; it was dangling around the neck of a food server. She also noticed a bizarre man with matted hair and a beard; he had a toothbrush sticking out of his boot. He wore no shirt, but a name tag attached to his bare chest identified him as "Harry." He had a CQ score of 88.9. He was standing next to his friend Henry, who was barefoot and had a CQ of 85.

The two men gawked at Carl's flashy pedometer watch, and Kara had a bad feeling.

Harry suddenly wigged out and pointed at Carl, shouting, "Elevator people. Elevator people."

Others in the church spotted Carl's watch and chimed in with the ghoulish mantra, "Elevator people. Elevator people. Elevator people… ."

Several vagrants pointed at Kara, Ellen, Angus, and the others, making it clear that they were aware of all eight "terrorist" intruders.

The entire room recited the creepy chant in unison, sounding like cult members.

A volunteer dialed 911. "Operator. It's an emergency. We're being invaded by elevator people."

Kara and the others hightailed it out of the building.

Harry and Henry pulled out knives and pursued the "terrorists" through the mostly empty streets. The chase extended past businesses, through intersections, and across a train track.

Bailey led the way. "Quick. In here." She motioned toward the Regal Hare Café, an upscale eatery with a notice attached to the door, "No shoes, no shirt, no service."

Then she slowed to a mannerly walk and whispered to her friends, "Be calm and confident. And don't look at anyone."

Bailey strolled into the restaurant with an air of self-assurance; the others followed.

"Our associates are already seated in the back," she said to a server near the door.

He nodded.

Shirtless Harry and shoeless Henry arrived two minutes later and attempted to enter the eatery but were blocked by a brawny maître d .

"I'm sorry, gentlemen. We have a dress code."

"They're getting away," Harry screamed, and pointed.

"You need to leave right now, sir," the maître d said. "Or I will have to call the police." He corralled the vagrants back to the sidewalk and extended his arms, blocking them from the entrance.

Meanwhile, Bailey led her friends through the kitchen and out the back door of the café, where they found themselves at a dead end. There was a brick wall to the left and a structure without windows or doors at the front. Bernie headed to the right, which seemed the only way out.

Bailey shouted, "No."

"No?" Bernie turned, confused.

"We're going down." Bailey struggled to slide the cover off a manhole, eventually getting assistance from Roger and Kara.

When the aperture was open, Bailey yelled, "Get in."

"You forget. I'm an old woman," Ellen griped as she climbed down the rusty ladder.

There were grumbles from the gang as they descended into the grungy tunnel, where they faced darkness and stench.

Roger, pulling up the rear, maneuvered the utility hole cover back into place only seconds before Harry and Henry arrived at the dead end with their knives.

The homeless men scanned the area, baffled. There was no sign of anyone.

"Where'd they go?" Harry asked. "Think they're still inside?"

"Beats me," Henry replied. "Let's skedaddle. I got a hankering for pancakes."

The vagrants stashed their weapons and headed back to the church.

Bailey led her friends through the foul-smelling tunnel to a nearby maintenance hole where they were able to emerge at street level.

"I'm impressed. You're quite the survivor, young lady," Carl said.

"I used to hang with pockets… before my baby was born."

"What are pockets?" Kara climbed out of the aperture and guided her friends toward a dumpster.

"Pickpockets. Purse snatchers. Cons. Sometimes you have to get away."

"You were a thief?" Ellen appeared shocked.

"No. I just hung with them. They kept a roof over my head. They were my homies."

The group reached the dumpster.

"Give me that." Kara snatched the watch off Carl's wrist.

"Hey, what are you doing?" Carl objected. "That's my pedometer watch."

"Sorry, Carl." She tossed it into the rubbish bin. "It's not a watch. It's a red flag. Everybody, give me your phones… Come on, right now."

Everybody reluctantly obeyed. Kara threw them into the dumpster. "Now, we need to formulate a plan. This is getting way too dangerous."

❧

Somewhere in the cosmos, the Council of the Universe was in session. Agent Bones was about to be thrust into the hot seat and asked about the progress of the Earthling Extermination Project.

"I'm loving this nose spray," a particle sitting on the front row beside Bones whispered.

He squirted a wad into his duck-billed schnozz.

"Where'd you get it?" Bones asked.

"People on Earth use it. I found it on a park bench."

"Do you think that's sanitary?" Bones shuddered.

The council finished roll call. Sheldon was munching on a three-foot-long tree branch.

"We have a quorum," the magistrate announced. "Now, Agent Bones, please step over to the exhibition area and give us an update on Phase One."

Bones did as he was instructed. He stood in an open area and moved a pointer at breakneck speed while numbers popped onto a floating board. Each scribble vanished a second after it was written.

Members of the council smiled as if they understood the data.

"Any images?" the magistrate asked.

Video of individuals in elevators materialized. It was laid out like a tic-tac-toe game with different people in each square. The humans were blind; many were screaming or crying.

The council members nodded and furrowed their brows, as if they were scientists examining human behavior.

"Did the subjects make it out of the elevator without incident?" the magistrate asked.

"Two fatalities. One person had a heart attack, and another took her own life."

"Not bad. Have there been any casualties since?"

"There've been 865 deaths, and several thousand are in prison."

"Could you show us the details, please?"

Bones again used a stick to point at fast-moving data on the board.

Suddenly, Sheldon's tree branch whacked into Darkon.

"Get your oak tree out of my face," Darkon barked, and turned to the head of the council. "He skewered me, magistrate."

"Put the branch away, Sheldon," she commanded.

"I'm surprised. It tastes pretty good." Sheldon took another bite of the branch.

"You are acting like a tadpole. You know the rule. No snacks at meetings. Put the branch away."

"Yes, magistrate." Sheldon complied with the order.

"Is there anything you'd like to add, Agent Bones?"

"The media are calling them 'elevator people.'"

"Elevator people. I like that," the magistrate added. "Do you need additional fortifications? We could grant you an extra twenty thousand combat particles to assist you with the project."

"I have enough troops for now, ma'am."

"Very well, Agent Bones. You may sit. Now councilmembers, we will be moving this meeting over to the planet Trion. There is an urgent situation that needs to be addressed."

Bones retook his seat in the front row. Then the particles in the room disappeared and reappeared in the Trion desert.

Chapter Four

ONE MAN'S VATE IS ANOTHER MAN'S MATE

After escaping from the vagrants who had identified them as elevator people, the eight brainstormed for an hour and then hatched a plan on how to survive the two weeks, mapping out the best way to lie low until the all-important date of July fourth. Everyone believed if they ran out the clock, they would eventually be transported back to their regular lives.

The first item on their to-do list was to locate a clueless person who would exchange their antique currency for modern-day cash. Although they had a meager $165, they needed at least some 2125 funds to carry out the rest of their plan.

Kara and Ellen were deemed the most innocent looking, so they were chosen to visit businesses until they found the "right employee" to make the swap.

The "right employee" was an individual who knew nothing about elevator people—someone who never watched the news.

After a couple of failures, and frankly close calls, Kara and Ellen sashayed into the Continental Gold and Silver Exchange. They found a sales clerk who was more interested in yoga and hip-hop than politics and current events.

When Kara mentioned "elevator people" in passing, the clerk said he had heard the phrase but did not know what it meant.

That was all Kara needed to hear. The funds were exchanged without incident.

The second item on the list was to get clothing that would allow them to fit in and aid them in getting hired. They needed to find jobs that would pay cash daily, which was crucial to procuring food and staying off the streets at night.

The eight found the outfits they needed at the Goodwill Thrift Shop for pennies on the dollar.

The next order of business was to alter the expiration dates on their driver's licenses. The eight crowded into a gas station restroom where they used correction fluid, a red pen, and a ruler to doctor the licenses. They also smudged brown paint—resembling dirt—over some of the dates to render the figures unreadable.

Then they visited a copy shop and created résumés. They invented cities, dates, and previous employment, figuring their lies would not be exposed until after July fourth.

The contact number for the primary reference on the résumés matched the number for the phone booth located next to the Zelles Hotel. Carl volunteered to monitor that booth and pretend to be the person listed on the paperwork.

The eight planned to search for jobs the following day, but in the meantime, they needed to find a free place to sleep for the night. They did not want to deplete their limited funds.

Roger had an idea. He led the others to the gray home with white shutters where the AAA Staging Company truck had been parked. He had seen it when walking to the library. There was an open house sign in the front yard, which bore the real estate agent's name, Gary House.

It was an unusual property in that the style was less Luddite and more modern—in fact, it was reminiscent of construction from the 2020s.

The eight hid in an adjacent wooded area teeming with American beech trees, tall grass, and giant ferns. The greenery was dense and abundant, providing excellent cover while allowing them to monitor the gray dwelling.

After a lengthy wait, a vehicle pulled up to the curb. A family climbed out of the car, clearly planning to attend the open house.

Roger grabbed Kara's hand and told her to play along.

They dashed toward the home, beating the family to the door, where they were greeted by Realtor Gary who wore a cartoon necktie, had a bouncy personality, and sported a CQ score of 25.3. He handed Roger and Kara a property flyer.

"Welcome. I'm Gary House. And yes, that's my real name. Would you please sign in?" Gary presented them with a visitor registry attached to a clipboard.

"Sure." Roger signed the fake name, "Harry Potter."

"This is my wife, Mr. House. We're just looky-loos. That's what you call people like us, right?"

Gary laughed.

"You don't need to waste time on us. You've got some solid buyers." Roger pointed at the family that was waiting to enter. He whispered to Gary, "They told me they plan to make an offer."

Gary perked up. "Really?" Then he directed his attention to

the family. "Welcome. Would you please sign in? My name is Gary House, and yes, that's my real name."

Roger bolted from room to room, while Kara tagged along. The place was decorated with a soft palette of bone gray, white, pale green, and baby pink. It was, without a doubt, unoccupied, as evidenced by the lack of possessions other than some large pieces of furniture and a few lamps and vases.

Kara kept asking Roger what he was looking for, but he did not answer. He was too frenzied, too immersed in what seemed to be an investigation. He tried to open the window in the master suite, but it was stuck, so he ducked into the master bath, unlocked that window, opened it, and then closed it. He did not refasten it.

"Roger, what are you doing?" Kara asked.

Again, she received no answer.

Roger was ready to leave and said good-bye to Realtor Gary, who told him to call if he had any questions.

Gary presented his business card, which Roger crammed into his pocket.

Roger and Kara rejoined the others in the wooded area. They watched and waited. Eventually, Gary closed up; he put his sign inside the house, locked the front door, and drove away.

It was beginning to get dark when the eight climbed over the fence into the backyard of the staged house. They crawled through the unlocked bathroom window. Once inside, Roger noticed Gary's open house sign, leaning against a wall near the front door.

"There's one cardinal rule," Roger said to the others. "No lights. Understand? There are four bedrooms. All double beds. Two people per room, but someone can sleep on the couch if you absolutely can't stand your roommate."

"This reminds me of the time I was in a thicket in Zambia," Carl reminisced. "Got kidnapped by a tribesman and locked in a dark shed. I broke free and killed that native with my cheese knife. They called me the Great Zambini back then."

Everyone stared at Carl like he was crazy.

"I thought The Great Zambini was a magician," Kara said.

"No. It was me."

"So, Roger… you say no lights." Ellen changed the subject. "Are we supposed to stumble around in the dark?"

"You're supposed to go right to sleep because we have to be out of here at dawn. It'll be a full day tomorrow. We have to get jobs. By the way, don't dirty up the place."

Bernie and Carl entered one room, and Ellen and Bailey took another. Angus and Keiko snagged a third bedroom. Roger and Kara were left with the master suite.

"It's just you and me…" Roger said. "Unless you can't stand your roommate."

"I'll try to tolerate you," she quipped.

In the bedroom, Roger removed his jacket and got into bed, facing away from Kara's side.

Kara stared at him, wishing he was interested, but then lay down with her back to him.

Hours passed. Everyone was asleep, except Angus, who got up at 4:15 a.m. and turned on a lamp. He plopped down in an armchair, put his filthy feet on a white ottoman, and flipped through *House & Home* magazine.

The illumination woke Roger, who stormed into Angus's room. "What are you doing? I said no lights."

"I couldn't sleep," Angus grumbled.

"You want to get us kicked out?"

"Screw you, Roger. You're not gonna tell me what to do. You're a fucking tyrant."

"Beat it, Roger. Leave my brother alone." Keiko sat up in bed.

Kara and the others were awakened by the commotion and appeared in the doorway.

"Look what you did." Roger tried to rub the dirt off the ottoman.

"Who cares?" Angus replied. "You're making a big stink about nothing."

Roger shut off the bedroom lamp but noticed a flashing squad car light outside the window. "Shit. I bet the neighbors called the cops. I'll handle it. Everybody, grab your stuff and get out the window. I'll meet up with you at the hotel."

There was a knock and then a second knock. Roger donned his jacket, turned on the living room light, took a deep breath, and answered the door.

Two officers, a male and a female, stood on the porch. In front of the male, the equation was "CQ = 76." But it was different with the female. In front of her, the equation was "Cruelty Quotient = 97.8. Extreme Caution!" Roger was flabbergasted. He could not believe it. The mystery of "CQ" had been solved.

He wondered if this cop was into police brutality. Perhaps she abused children, stalked boyfriends, or shot puppies in the face. Maybe she was a serial killer. Anything was possible. Roger figured the CQ was designed to alert elevator people about stranger danger, to caution them about louts with high scores. Although he was uneasy, especially concerning the female officer, Roger tried to act calm and confident.

The lady cop asked, "Do you live here, sir?"

"No. I'm the Realtor, Gary House. And yes, that's my real name." Roger chuckled.

"Do you have any identification?"

Roger pulled Gary's business card from his pocket and handed it to her.

In the distance, he caught a glimpse of his friends scooting down the street and out of sight.

Roger pointed at the "Gary House" sign, leaning against the wall.

"I was doing an open house today, but this place got a little messy. You know how those looky-loos are. I have a showing this morning at five a.m. Some buyer wants to see the place before work, so I rushed back here to tidy up. We Realtors are on call twenty-four hours a day. And I gave up being a lawyer for this. I hope I didn't disturb any neighbors."

The cops seemed bothered by the "lawyer" reference, and the female officer returned the business card.

"No. Everything's fine. Good luck with your buyer," she said.

The cops departed.

&

The sun was rising when Roger caught up with the others in front of the Zelles Hotel.

"Hallelujah." Ellen gave Roger a hug. "You're not in the pokey."

"Nope," Roger said. "But we lost our dormitory thanks to Mother Teresa."

"It was a dumb idea to stay there in the first place," Angus griped.

Roger briefed the group about his findings related to the CQ equation.

Everyone expressed surprise. There were various theories about what it meant to have a high cruelty quotient, but everyone agreed it was not a good thing.

"One of us needs to find a job that will give us a place to crash," Kara said. "Like a hotel."

"I could give it a whirl," Ellen replied. "In my thirties, I worked at Caesars Palace."

"There's an employment agency two blocks over. I'm gonna go for a research job," Kara said.

"I'll try the employment agency, too," Roger added.

"I'll park myself at the phone booth," Carl stated. "In case any bosses call. I'm pretty darn good on the blower."

Kara eyeballed Angus and Keiko. "What about you two? We expect you to pull your weight."

"We need food," Roger said. "Maybe the Mother Teresas could get a job at a restaurant or grocery store."

"Stop fucking calling us that," Angus shouted.

Everyone except the Mother Teresas laughed.

"We'll meet back here at 5:15," Roger said.

"Roger that, boss." Carl fired off a military salute and headed toward the phone booth.

Everyone else wandered off to find work.

◈

Kara arrived back at the Zelles Hotel in the late afternoon and found Carl napping on the concrete.

She joked, "Gee, Carl. Looks like you've had a rough day."

Carl woke and clambered to his feet. "Must have dozed off."

"It's 5:30. No one else is back?"

"They're at Paradise Mattress." Carl handed Kara a business card for the store. "Bernie hit the jackpot. He got a sales job, plus they gave him a key to open in the morning and close at night."

"You're kidding? That's fantastic." Kara headed toward the mattress store but turned when she noticed Carl was not following. "You coming?"

"I have to wait for the spoiled brats. They haven't shown."

Paradise Mattress was a small business in a strip mall. Signage on the storefront read "Open," "Free Frame with any

Purchase," and "Discount on King Beds." In the parking lot was a delivery truck bearing the company name. Kara entered the store's showroom to find wood flooring, a cashier's desk, and an estimated twenty beds, as well as Bernie, Roger, Ellen, and Bailey, hanging out on a mattress, gabbing.

Kara realized this was not an average mattress store. The place was laid out like a Piet Mondrian masterpiece. Mondrian was a twentieth-century Dutch painter and the king of abstract art; he used squares and rectangles as if they were going out of style.

She figured the mattress store owner had artistic aspirations. Maybe he was a connoisseur of collage, cubism, or even synthetic cubism. Perhaps he was a regular visitor at the Museum of Modern Art in New York City—that is, if the place still existed.

Kara approached her friends and high-fived the man of the hour. "Bernie. This is amazing."

"You haven't seen the best part." Bernie led her to the back room. It was an enormous, windowless break room with a television, a clock, a bathroom, and a refrigerator, as well as additional mattresses.

Kara asked Bernie how he landed the job, and he dove into the story.

&

Bernie explained how he had walked into Paradise Mattress that morning and had run into the elderly store owner, Mr. Pebblebrook, who had a CQ score of 38.5.

"Did John send you?" Mr. Pebblebrook asked.

"No. My name's Bernie. I'm looking for a job."

"John didn't send you? He was supposed to send someone over this morning."

"No. I'm Bernie."

Mr. Pebblebrook seemed distressed as he wandered behind the checkout counter. "I knew it. I should never trust John. Have you ever sold mattresses?"

"No. I sold used cars after high school. I've also worked at an auto parts store."

"It's not easy to sell used cars. Why do you look like you've been vandalized?"

"Excuse me."

"You look like a graffiti wall."

"Oh, you mean the tattoos. I'm a responsible person. I made dean's list in college."

Mr. Pebblebrook stared at Bernie long and hard. "I'm in a bind. My only two salesmen quit last week. My wife has cancer."

"I'm sorry."

"She wants to go to Italy and doesn't have a lot of time. We have tickets to leave tonight. I hate to shut down the store… but… I guess I have no choice."

"I could handle it for you, sir. I'm an excellent salesman." Bernie motioned toward a bed on display. "This is a hybrid design composed of organic wool and latex." Then he pointed to a different mattress. "And this particular brand has high-quality lumbar support, and it was designed by a team of physicians. It soothes chronic back pain."

"How do you know that?"

"My mom had spine problems. She tried a different mattress every month until she found the right one. If you close down the store, you'll be leaving money on the table and disappointing your customers. They may never come back."

Mr. Pebblebrook seemed hesitant. "Hmm… Well. I don't know. I don't know anything about you."

"You wouldn't know anything about John's guy. And John's a flake, so anyone he sends would probably be a flake, too."

"That's a good point. Do you think you could handle it by yourself for ten days? Until I get back?"

"Yes, sir. I definitely can."

"You'd have to be open every day from ten to five."

"I can do that."

Mr. Pebblebrook stared at Bernie. "Please don't steal my mattresses."

"I won't. I promise."

"Okay. I'm gonna take a chance on you. Let me show you how everything works."

❧

Bernie, Roger, Ellen, Bailey, and Kara were in the mattress store break room.

Bernie pointed out the refrigerator was partially stocked and pulled a handgun from a drawer. "We've got protection from those evil elevator people."

Everyone laughed.

"I have some good news, too. I'm officially a technician at the Worthington Research Institute, starting tomorrow. And I talked them into paying me by the day." Kara took a bow. "Thank you. Thank you. No applause needed."

"That's great," Ellen replied. "Bailey and I haven't found anything yet."

Kara turned to Roger. "What about you?"

He ignored the question and opened the fridge door. "Is there any fruit?"

"Come on," Kara continued. "It can't be that bad."

Roger hemmed and hawed, but finally spilled the humiliating beans. "I have an interview tomorrow at the Big Tractor Store."

"The Big Tractor Store?" Kara replied. "Doing what?"

Roger once again hesitated. "Senior gopher."

"Senior gopher? That's an outrage. You're not even qualified to be a junior gopher."

Everyone laughed.

"I'm sorry. I don't mean to make fun of you. Let's all congratulate Chief Rodent."

There was applause, snickering, a slap on the back, and a "Hooray, Chief Rodent."

"Okay, you've had your fun, Miss Hotsy-Totsy Research Technician." Roger tackled Kara, and they fell onto a mattress, laughing.

Kara was thrilled that Roger was starting to be playful with her. He was no longer treating her like a department store mannequin.

A couple of hours passed. Roger was munching on an apple while Kara, Ellen, Bernie, and Bailey were scarfing down cookies, guzzling Coke, and watching a rerun of *I Love Lucy* on the break room TV. They could not get a clear picture on a news channel.

Kara grabbed a fourth cookie. "Time travel sure is fattening. Too bad it's not quantum physics. I could be Schrodinger's cat. I could be both fat and skinny at the same time."

"Plus, Kara…" Roger replied. "You could be both talking and saying nothing at the same time. Oh wait, you already do that."

Everyone laughed.

"Ha, ha." Kara smiled.

There was a banging. Everyone ventured into the showroom, where they saw Carl and Keiko through the storefront. Keiko was pounding on the glass in a panic. Carl looked freaked out, too, which was unusual for the admittedly crazy, but usually mellow, former soldier.

Roger unlocked the door.

"I barely got away." Keiko was out of breath. "They're

monsters. They grabbed Angus. They said we were elevator people and called the police. It's like a cult."

"What?" Kara asked.

"They're murdering people. Eating them. They're gonna eat Angus. I just know it."

"Eating people?' Kara replied. "That can't be right."

"Where?" Roger asked.

"At the First Street Deli. We have to help him."

"Wait here." Roger ran to the break room.

Kara wondered if Keiko was mistaken. Maybe he only *thought* he saw people being killed. Maybe he was hallucinating due to the pressure related to time travel and being in Luddite land. Or maybe his eyesight had gone all wonky again, like it had in the elevator.

For a fleeting second, Kara thought about staying put and embracing the safety of the mattress store. But it was only for a fleeting second. She knew she had to help Angus. Her identity revolved around assisting those in need. Her life's mission was to aid the oppressed, the voiceless, the marginalized, and the forgotten. Plus, she was accustomed to danger. Her journeys to the Middle East had, on occasion, required dodging bullets, bombs, and angry militants.

Roger returned with the gun.

Kara and the others hurried toward the First Street Deli.

Chapter Five

A KNUCKLE SANDWICH

Although darkness had descended on Baltimore, it was a full two hours before curfew. The seven were crowded behind a wide-trunked tree and some bushes in a pocket park. The park was across the street from the First Street Deli and equipped with a swing set, a slide, a teeter-totter, and a sand pit.

"I think there are two classes of people," Keiko said. "The weak ones are slaves. They're made into food. Angus isn't strong. He puts on a good show, but he's really, really weak."

"You guys stay put. No need to risk everyone getting caught." Roger checked to be sure he had bullets in the handgun.

He was proud of himself; he was tapping into his new unafraid and unscripted self. The old Roger would have let someone else step up to the plate and be the hero. In a sense, he was thankful for

Joan's harsh words. They had transformed him into a better person. He would try, going forward, to avoid being boring and milquetoast. In fact, at that very moment, he felt like Superman, like he could zoom off to a ski resort in Switzerland once the time travel ordeal was over and things were back to normal.

Roger bolted across the street to the deli and peered through the storefront. The place looked like a 1950s diner. It had a black-and-white checkered floor, a jukebox, red booths, and a counter with stools. It was packed with customers and seemed quite ordinary. But when Roger scanned the room more closely, he saw something confusing. It appeared that a partially eviscerated woman was being roasted on a skewer behind a glass partition. At the very least, the mass of browned flesh was shaped like a female torso, and Roger couldn't figure out what else it could be.

The sight reminded him of a high-end Baltimore restaurant that specialized in charcuterie and cheeses, which he had once visited with Joan. The place brazenly displayed a full-size, cooked pig on a rotisserie behind a similar glass divide—head, snout, tail, and all. At the time, Roger was shocked that patrons at this top Michelin-rated eatery did not seem bothered by the gruesome sight, including his admittedly less-emotional wife. But he was bothered, so he scarfed down his food, quickly paid the bill, and never returned.

A squad car stopped in front of the First Street Deli. Luckily, Roger could think on his feet and jumped into action. He waved his arms, pretending to flag down the vehicle. Two officers got out. Cop Larry had a CQ score of 70.4, and Cop Stan had a score of 64.7. Larry removed his Baltimore Police windbreaker and tossed it into the cruiser through an open window. Then he adjusted his uniform cap.

Roger ran to the two men. "Officers. Officers. I'm so glad you're here. I'm the one who called about the elevator person.

He escaped. He went down the street to Walter's Café." He pointed at the café at the end of the block. "Be careful and go slowly because he has a gun."

Cop Stan smiled. "Thanks. We'll handle it. You need to get off the street, sir."

"Sure thing," Roger replied.

Roger watched the two cops head down the sidewalk and grabbed the windbreaker from the police vehicle. He put it on, making himself look official. He entered the deli with a John Wayne swagger. Customers stopped talking and stared at him; they had CQs that ranged from 44 to 99. For scores greater than 90, "Cruelty Quotient," was written out, followed by the phrase, "Extreme Caution!"

"Detective Potter here," Roger announced to the room. "Someone called about an elevator person."

Randolph Schmidt, the owner of the deli, stepped forward. Floating in front of him was "Cruelty Quotient = 96.8. Extreme Caution!"

"Yeah. There were two," Randolph said. "One's in the freezer. The other got away."

"You didn't kill him, did you?" Roger asked. "I mean, I need to get him to fess up about his buddy."

"He's still alive unless he's frozen to death." Randolph laughed, as did a handful of customers and employees.

Randolph led Roger into the kitchen, which resembled the sort of food prep area that might have been found at a restaurant in 2025. The appliances, counters, pots, pans, trays, cabinetry, ladles, knives, and other accoutrements did not look primitive. They appeared to be top-of-the-line; there was a lot of stainless steel and gadgetry.

Three cooks wore white shirts, aprons, and white hats. They had CQ scores over 96.

Roger walked past a curious collection of canned food,

stacked in a tidy pyramid on a countertop. The cans were identical, and the label read "Boneless Pickled Feet." The image on the cans depicted the lower extremities of a person—from the ankle down to the toes.

Then Roger looked closely at the cuisine that was being prepared, and he was once again bewildered. He saw a container of what looked like human toes, although the nails had been removed. He also noticed what he believed to be human elbows with garnish and human hands in a casserole dish covered with grape tomatoes and white sauce. One chef was putting what looked like finger joints between two pieces of bread, thus making a knuckle sandwich in the literal sense.

Roger wondered if he was misinterpreting his surroundings. Maybe there was a fad in this society—albeit a peculiar one—to make food look like people's body parts in the same way that a cook might carve cucumbers and carrots to resemble garden flowers. Or... perhaps it was similar to how a server might twist aluminum foil into animal shapes for an artsy to-go bag of leftovers.

Roger thought, *Maybe Keiko confused a creative presentation of food with something more nefarious. Maybe Angus's life is not in jeopardy after all.*

Randolph led Roger from the kitchen to a walk-in freezer, which was when Roger realized the dreadful truth. This was not a culinary trick. There was no sleight of hand. Keiko was right: People were being eaten. Roger saw wall-to-wall frozen, dead bodies hanging from hooks. It looked like a serial killer's trophy room.

Angus was curled up on the floor in a corner, shivering and terrified.

Roger tried to set aside his shock and revulsion; he needed to act like a cop.

"I'll get him down to the station and interrogate the hell out of him. He'll give it up. They always do." Roger then spoke to Angus, "I'm Detective Potter. Now get up. You're coming with me.

Angus stood, trembling, and took baby steps toward Roger.

"Let's go." Roger tugged on Angus's arm.

"Don't you have handcuffs?" Randolph asked.

"Nah. My partner's got them. We were in the midst of a drug raid on Fifth and Highland when I got your call. But don't worry. These vates are pretty easy to keep under control. Plus, I'll break his face if he tries to run."

Unbeknownst to Roger, the other six—Kara, Bailey, Carl, Bernie, Ellen, and Keiko—had moved down to the storefront and were looking through the glass. They were mortified. Not only did they spot the roasted female corpse on the skewer, they also saw plates of food on a table, consisting of human ears with peas and a braised human foot next to a serving of potato salad. They hid in the shadows when they noticed Larry and Stan were doubling back.

Larry and Stan stormed inside the deli, just as Roger, Angus, and Randolf were entering the dining room from the kitchen.

The customers were clearly skilled at detecting vates, because they pointed at Roger and Angus and chanted in unison, "Elevator people, Elevator people, Elevator people, Elevator people…"

They came off as robotic and soulless. Their monotone voices sounded sinister and creepy.

Roger motioned at the corpse on the skewer and screamed, "Look at that! You're murderers. You're fucking Nazis. All of you."

Cop Stan drew his weapon and yelled, "Freeze."

Randolph tried to grab Roger, but Roger knuckled him in the face and hightailed it back into the kitchen with Angus.

Kara, still positioned outside the storefront, noticed Roger was in trouble and figured she needed to help him. She knew of an alley behind the establishment and assumed he might use it to escape.

She jumped into Stan and Larry's squad car, but the key was not in the ignition. She frantically searched the vehicle, finding it tucked under the floor mat on the driver's side. In her panic, she dropped the key into the gap between the center console and the seat. She eventually fished it out, aware that she was losing precious time. Kara started the engine and veered into a side alley, grazing three trash cans that went gyrating into a wall.

The deli kitchen was becoming a full-fledged mess. It looked like the aftermath of a food fight. Roger flung pots, pans, and a tossed green salad at Randolph and two vigilante customers with CQs close to 100. The frightened cooks hid in a pantry.

Then Roger threw forks, spoons, and carrots at Cop Larry, who slipped and fell to the ground.

Roger heaved the container of toes at Cop Stan, who shot off his gun erratically. Bullets flew in every direction but did not hit anyone.

Roger pulled out his revolver and fired back to buy time while he and Angus barreled out the back door into the alley. They sprinted past dumpsters as well as abandoned tires and other rubbish.

Cop Stan peeped out to see that the vates were far in the distance. He motioned for the others to follow.

The police officers, Randolph, and the vigilantes raced down the alley.

This is when Kara arrived in the squad car. She thought about running over the cops and their cohorts and even veered toward them with a mischievous glint in her eye. But at the last second, she thought better of it and zoomed around them. She caught up with Roger and Angus.

"Get in," she shouted.

Angus hesitated.

Roger stuffed him through the open passenger window, jumped in the back, and off they went.

The cops shot at the vehicle as it sped away with Angus's feet dangling out the window.

᪥

Police detective Julie Ponderosa was sixty years old, five feet tall, and 240 pounds. In truth, her weight fluctuated between 236 and 253; it all depended on how much meat and potatoes she'd consumed that month.

Julie liked eating more than romance, although she'd had intercourse only a handful of times in her younger years. As a preteen, she had taken opera lessons from a portly, middle-aged man who had informed her that food was better than sex.

"Spaghetti and meatballs. It's much better," her teacher had said. "And Wisconsin butter burgers with two teaspoons of soy sauce."

It was a mystifying thing to tell a twelve-year-old girl, and she had never forgotten the comment. She'd shrugged it off as a lame attempt to secure a dinner companion. She would have dubbed him a dirty old man if he'd said it the other way around.

Julie had never married and lived in a townhouse that she had refinanced twice to get cash to pay for her most financially wasteful hobby: costume collecting. She regularly spent thousands of dollars on spiffy garments that were purportedly worn by nobility: queens, kings, empresses, princesses, and dukes. She would dress up as a male or female member of a royal family, depending on her mood.

She had each piece altered to fit her body, which cost a pretty penny. She liked the whalebone hoop skirts and bustles that had been worn by females as well as the capes, tunics, and fur outerwear that males had worn.

Julie was a fan of ornate fabric and reveled in the rich color palette of gold, violet, red, and purple. The outfits made her feel special—regal—like a person of privilege. Of course, it was not odd to collect costumes due to the pervasive Luddite culture. Everything old was new again, or at least fashionable again.

She also had an extensive collection of swords, although many—if not all—were replicas of weapons used by former royals. Julie was never quite sure if the sellers of these relics had been on the up-and-up about their authenticity. She would regularly wear a scabbard or sheath attached to her belt at work; this was essentially a leather piece of protective casing that held the sword.

It had been common in past eras for kings, princes, and other aristocrats to take swords into battle, and Julie equated her detective job with "going into battle." She routinely carried her sword along with her standard-issue handgun, which had its own holster. When her workmates weren't calling her "the resident swashbuckler," they described her as a "brutal broad." Julie was the toughest cookie in the bakehouse. She had a CQ score of 94.9. Most of the officers were afraid of her.

Julie's life was her work. She would don costumes in the privacy of her home but could never get the latest investigation out of her head. She was always in case-solving mode, mulling over clues and ruminating on possible suspects.

She was also rather tech-savvy for a person in 2125. Despite the public's general disapproval of technology and the laws that prohibited it, Julie knew it could help with her job—that is, if it was made legal. She was always complaining about technophobes. Most of her colleagues fit the label quite well.

Julie entered the First Street Deli, wearing her sheath and sword, where she found Randolph, the two cops, and a handful of other employees. The place was closed for business due to the damage done by the vate incident. There were broken dishes, food on the floor, and an appearance of general disarray.

"I'm Detective Ponderosa. I handle vate cases in Baltimore. Can you tell me what happened?"

Randolph shared the sordid story about the evil elevator people who had invaded his humble mom-and-pop business.

❦

The eight were in the break room at the mattress store, watching a rerun of *Seinfeld*. Kara was playing nurse, tending to Roger's cuts and bruises, while Angus sat alone in the corner, still numb from his brush with death.

"Are you sure we can't get the news?" Kara asked.

Bernie flipped channels, finding only two with a clear picture. "It's either a game show or the sitcom channel."

Then he landed on a local news program, but it was snowy. Although it had poor reception, the eight could make out the image of a reporter, and they could hear her. She was discussing a local arrest over bribery charges.

"See, it's no good." Bernie started to switch back to *Seinfeld*.

"No, leave it," Kara said.

Bernie shrugged and sat down.

Roger checked the fridge to find it empty, and turned to Bernie. "Can you give me some cash so I can pick up a couple of cheese pizzas?"

"I don't have any money."

"Why not? Aren't you getting paid?" Roger asked.

"Yeah, but not by the day. Mr. Pebblebrook said we'd square up when he gets back."

Everyone groaned.

"How are we supposed to eat?" Ellen asked.

"Maybe we could borrow some cash from the register?" Roger turned to Bernie again. "We can put it back later."

"This place takes only credit cards. The register's empty."

Everyone groaned again.

Roger pulled out thirty bucks. "This is all that's left, and we need to save some for tomorrow. I'll pick up bread and peanut butter for dinner. We're gonna have to ration until Kara and I get paid."

The TV reporter pointed at a graph of crime statistics. "Murder rates have increased dramatically in the region."

"Gee, I wonder why?" Kara screamed at the set. "Maybe cause you're eating people."

"I don't think she can hear you," Roger joked.

"They either want to arrest us as elevator people or turn us into the Denny's dinner special," Ellen added.

The reporter continued, "We have breaking news on local terrorism. Details after this message."

"Oh, goody. We're up next," Kara quipped.

There was a commercial for the WinRight grocery store, accompanied by a catchy jingle. There were images of fruits, vegetables, cereal boxes, and dead people floating in what appeared to be a huge lobster tank. Shoppers smiled as they pushed their carts past the corpses.

"Oh, my word," Ellen exclaimed.

"We're in the effing twilight zone," Keiko said.

"How many more days till this nightmare is over?" Bailey placed her face in her hands.

The commercial ended, and the reporter appeared next to a caption that read "Vate Update."

Bernie increased the volume on the set.

"Tonight, two elevator people smashed up Baltimore's First Street Deli and shot at police and customers," the reporter said. "A third one stole a police car. The vehicle was later found abandoned in a school parking lot. No one was killed or injured. Randolph Schmidt is the owner of the deli."

Randolph appeared on camera. "We're peace-loving folks, but these vates are the devil. They hate our way of life. They're fanatics. They've gotta be stopped."

The journalist came back on-screen. "These terrorists are at large and have a gun. If you have any information about their whereabouts, please call 911. They are considered dangerous."

⋘

It was an emergency meeting to discuss the Earthling Extermination Project. The magistrate was not present, but all other Council of the Universe members were seated. The audience section of the venue was only partially full because there had been insufficient communication about the proceeding. The law mandated appropriate notification, usually seventy-two hours, to facilitate public access to legislative discussions and decision making. However, exceptions were made for urgent situations, such as this one.

Bones sat in the rear of the room. He finished rubbing down his torso with Brasso metal polish, and then he extracted tweezers and a compact mirror, which he used to pluck unwanted hairs from his cheeks and chin. His precision was spot-on; he was like a top-notch surgeon when it came to self-care.

Darkon banged a gavel furiously on the judge's bench. "Order. Order. This meeting's called to order."

"But the magistrate hasn't arrived," Sheldon spoke out.

"I'm second-in-command. You're third, so you should shut your fat beak." Darkon pounded the gavel another half a dozen times.

"She'll be here soon." Sheldon tried again. "The traffic on the Constellation Highway is a bear."

"Oh, stop being a gasbag." Darkon stood and scanned the chamber. "Agent Bones, where the hell are you?"

"You're in a particularly grumpy mood today," Sheldon noted.

"Well, there was a lot of traffic on the Constellation Highway," Darkon huffed.

Bones quickly slipped the tweezers and mirror into his tiny travel bag and rushed to the presentation area.

"So, what's the emergency?" Darkon asked.

"All the elevator people in Liechtenstein are in jail," Bones said.

"Never heard of it. It must be the size of a beady bug eye."

"It's in Europe," Bones spoke.

Darkon reviewed a map. "Oh, it's just some landlocked microstate that no one gives a diddle about."

"There won't be any specimens to carry out Phase One or Phase Two," Bones interjected.

The magistrate hurried into the meeting and took her usual position.

"Can't we just kill off the whole region? Let's take a vote," Darkon stated.

"Give me the gavel," the magistrate commanded.

Darkon complied.

"We are not killing off any regions. Now, what's the emergency, Agent Bones?"

"All the elevator people in Liechtenstein are in jail. There's nobody to complete Phase One or Phase Two."

"That could pose a problem," the magistrate replied. "What's the population?"

"35,261."

Sheldon raised his hand, and the magistrate motioned for him to speak.

"Should we ready the elevators for another batch of random specimens?"

"No. I think we should redraw the map. Some of the elevator people in Switzerland and Austria can handle the load in Liechtenstein. How does the Council feel about that?"

Everyone, except Darkon, raised their arms in a show of support.

"Make the arrangements, Agent Bones," the magistrate ordered.

"But… I don't think that'll work," Bones said. "There won't be enough particles or time or—"

The magistrate interrupted. "Agent Bones! You are not to argue with the Council. It's your responsibility to make sure this goes smoothly."

"Might be easier to kill off the whole region," Bones mumbled.

"What did you say?" The magistrate appeared livid. "Are you being cheeky?"

"No. I didn't say anything. I'm sorry, ma'am. I'll handle it." Bones moped out of the room, figuring Liechtenstein was doomed.

Chapter Six

EYES WIDE SHUT

It was morning. The showroom at Paradise Mattress looked like a teen slumber party. Each person's belongings were sprawled out on and around his or her particular bed. There were ample pillows and blankets, purchased from the Salvation Army. The shades were closed so potential customers could not see that the room was, in effect, a dormitory rather than a shop.

On the previous day, each elevator person had nabbed a bed that conformed to his or her comfort level. It was like *Goldilocks* minus the Little Wee Bear, the Middle-Sized Bear, and the Great Big Bear. Some mattresses were deemed too soft, others too hard, and finally, some were just right.

Everyone was still asleep on their "just right mattress," except for Kara and Roger, who were dressed and ready for the work day. Kara wore her lucky red scarf.

"My interview's thirty minutes outside the city, but I can give you a lift," Roger said to Kara.

They headed out the door and climbed into the company delivery truck, emblazoned with the words "Paradise Mattress."

After a five-minute drive, Roger stopped at the Worthington Research Institute.

Kara got out, closed the truck door, and spoke through the open window. "Good luck with your interview. Today big tractors. Tomorrow the world."

Roger laughed. "Hey Kara… about lunch. Don't eat anything that looks like meat."

"I've been wanting to go vegan for years. This could be the right time." She smiled and headed into the business.

No one was in the reception area, but Kara took a seat anyway.

Eventually, the owner of the establishment appeared. Her name was Dr. Leila Dijon, and she was an uptight rule follower with a CQ of 100. She was the type of person who would not— or perhaps could not—show emotion. She was like a cyborg, often viewed by her comrades as part machine because of her uncharitable, callous, and mechanical nature. Some people joked that society's tech-hating crowd should have banned her existence.

"Are you Dr. Carson?" Dr. Dijon questioned.

"Yes."

"I'm Dr. Leila Dijon."

"Dijon? Like the mustard?" Kara asked.

"Yes. Follow me."

Dr. Dijon led Kara into a private office that had a desk, a bookcase, a cabinet with drawers, and a few chairs. Both women sat.

"I'd like to welcome you aboard."

"Thank you, Dr. Dijon."

"I understand your experience is with microbiology and cosmetic science." Dr. Dijon studied Kara's resume.

"Yes. I worked at a perfume company. I dealt with preservatives, gum, petrochemicals, balsam—."

Dr. Dijon interrupted her. "Have you ever done basic research?"

"I don't think so, but I'm a fast learner."

"We're starting you off in the filing room. I know it isn't glamorous, but our paperwork has gotten out of control. Within a day or so, we'll move you over to the laboratory."

Dr. Dijon led Kara down a sterile, white hallway into a research lab, where Kara froze in horror. She saw people—men, women, and children—in numbered cages. Some of the victims whimpered; all looked distraught. None had CQ scores.

A researcher named Olive with a CQ of 100 wore a white lab coat and hovered over a forty-year-old man shackled to a metal lab table. Olive poured a viscous liquid into the man's eyes; his eyes were held open by metal braces. He screamed in agony and squirmed, but his movements were limited due to the restraints. Kara was sickened and on the verge of tears, but knew she had to hide her empathy. She did not want to tip anyone off to her status as an elevator person.

Dr. Dijon calmly said, "This is Olive. She's working on a specimen now."

Olive and Dr. Dijon seemed numb to the victim's pain. They were nonchalant as if torture was routine, sanctioned, and simply part of the job.

"The Draize test is a staple of basic research," Dr. Dijon lectured Kara. "It tests the amount of toxic substance needed to inflict blindness or damage to the eye."

"Dr. Dijon?" Kara murmured.

"Yes?"

"I... I just want to make sure everything is being done legally," Kara stuttered.

"Of course it is." Dr. Dijon appeared offended. "We had an inspection last week. You sound like one of those—"

Kara was certain the next words out of her mouth would be "elevator people," so she quickly interrupted, "I figure everything is legal. It's just that I'm a by-the-book girl. I would never want to do anything improper."

"What exactly do you think we're doing that's improper?" Dr. Dijon sounded cross and scary.

Kara was in panic mode, thinking her cover was about to be blown. She scanned the room desperately until she caught sight of a donut on a plate.

"Um... well... Where I worked, we weren't allowed to eat in the lab."

Dr. Dijon honed in on the donut and smiled. "You're absolutely right, Dr. Carson." Then she turned her attention to Olive. "Olive, what's that donut doing here? No food in the laboratory."

"Yes, Doctor."

Olive took the plate out of the room.

Dr. Dijon turned to Kara. "I think you're going to be a valuable part of our little family." She led Kara to the filing room.

Piles of papers were stacked on chairs, a desk, and the floor. Filing cabinets lined the walls; some had open drawers, and folders were sticking out. The place was in disarray; it needed organization.

"Alan will be in to explain what you need to do," Dr. Dijon said, then departed.

Kara was distraught as she peered through a small window in the door, which provided a view of the laboratory, including the caged victims and the (possibly blind) man who was being tortured on the table.

It was not long before Alan arrived. He was a young man in a white lab coat with a CQ of 100. He explained the filing process.

Kara tried to absorb the instructions, but her anguish over the victims in the other room made it hard for her to concentrate. He told her that lunch was from eleven until noon.

After Alan left, Kara quickly resumed her spot at the small window. She saw five scientists, all with CQs of 100, hovering over two women, strapped to tables. The victims screamed and cried. She also saw Olive slide the Draize test victim into an incinerator; he was sobbing and begging for mercy.

Then poof. The man was silent. His flesh and organs had been reduced to ashes.

Kara realized that compassion was absent in this twisted world. The researchers were sadistic, or at best apathetic to the suffering of others—a mindset that she found incomprehensible. But one thing made sense: she understood why their cruelty quotients were sky-high.

All morning, Kara alternated her activity between her filing duties and peering out the window in the door. She felt compelled to see what her associates were doing. When it was eleven a.m., she watched Olive and Alan push the two females—who appeared to be deceased—into the incinerator. Then she heard them discuss swinging by a taco restaurant for lunch, and they headed out.

Kara tiptoed out of the filing room, scanning the lab to make sure all her associates were gone. She checked the ceiling and light fixtures for recording equipment and even asked the caged victims if there were any cameras in the room. No one answered, but some pleaded for assistance.

"Help," one woman cried.

"They're gonna kill me," a man said.

Most of the victims looked dejected, like they had given up on life.

Kara was almost in tears. "I'm so sorry this is happening to you. I'm so sorry. I don't know what to do. There's only one of me and so many of them."

Kara paced, unsure how to handle the situation.

She kept glancing at the clock as time ticked closer and closer to noon.

Eventually, she moved to cage number eight, occupied by ten children, all under the age of six. It was adjacent to a door with a sign that read "Emergency Exit Only. Alarm will sound if opened."

Kara once again swept the room to make sure none of the researchers were present, and then she opened the cage door.

"Come on," Kara said. "Don't be scared. Come on out. Come on. Come on out."

The victims seemed tentative, unsure whether to trust Kara, but they eventually edged out of the enclosure.

A pretty little female, who appeared to be about five, had an unsightly research gash on her neck.

Kara kneeled in front of her. "What's your name?"

The girl stared at Kara but did not speak. Kara figured she might not speak English. Perhaps she was from another country or had never been introduced to phonics. On the other hand, maybe she was mute or frozen with fear, worried that she was about to become a "specimen."

"Do you have a name?" Kara tried again, but there was no answer. "I'm gonna call you Angel."

Kara removed the embroidered red scarf from her neck and wrapped it around the small girl so the hideous blemish was no longer visible. The words "To Kara, our warrior. From your little lambs" were visible.

"This is my lucky scarf," she told the little one.

Angel smiled.

Then Kara spoke to the children outside the cage. "Now, I'm gonna open the door, and you're gonna run. Do you understand?"

There was no response.

Kara opened the emergency exit. Surprisingly, there was no alarm.

"Get out. Go. Go. Hurry up. Out." She quickly shoved Angel and the other children into the alley. Then she shut the door behind them.

Caged victims ratcheted up their cries for aid. Kara heard them say, "Help," "Please," "Over here," and "Don't forget about me."

Kara turned to everyone tearfully. "I promise. I will get all of you out, but you've got to be patient. I'm so sorry this is happening to you."

There were confused looks on the victims' faces.

"Do you understand?"

None of the victims replied.

Kara noticed it was almost noon, so she scurried back into the filing room and immersed herself in her work. It was not long before she heard displeased voices outside the door. She carefully peeped through the window to see Olive, Dr. Dijon, Alan, and several other scientists; they were agitated over the missing children. When Kara noticed Dr. Dijon moving in her direction, she jumped away from the window and pretended to be preoccupied.

Dr. Dijon peeped into the filing room. "Dr. Carson, do you know what happened to the specimens in cage eight?"

Kara mustered the most innocent expression possible. "I have no idea. But you'll be pleased. I'm getting a lot of work done today."

"Thank you, Dr. Carson."

Dr. Dijon left, and Kara let out a sigh of relief.

❧

Roger had a different sort of day. After dropping Kara off at Worthington Research, he drove to the Big Tractor Store, located in a semi-rural part of Maryland. It was a white building with slitty windows and an array of shiny, new farm equipment parked out front.

He entered the structure to find rakes, lawn mowers, power tools, welding equipment, fencing, ladders, grain carts, and tractors. There were displays of caps and T-shirts in various colors, adorned with an assortment of farm-related insignias.

Marlin, an employee, was organizing fertilizer on a shelf. He had a CQ of 88.9.

"Hi," Roger said. "I'm here for the job interview."

"Oh, gee," Marlin replied. "That's right. The senior errand boy."

He yelled toward the back of the store, "Bob, the guy's here for the gopher job."

Bob's voice shot back, "Lance is gonna handle it. Send him across the street."

Marlin turned to Roger. "Sorry to drag you all the way out here, but Bob's got it covered. I could hook you up across the street if you really need work."

"Across the street?"

"Yeah. We own Happy Farms. Always need processors."

"Do you pay cash by the day?"

"Ah… you're one of those. Down on your luck, huh? Sure, we can do that. Lots of our boys get paid at the end of the day. Just go across the street and ask for JP. Tell him Marlin sent you."

Roger left, thrilled that he had landed a job without an interview. He thought it would be a breeze to cover food and expenses for the next two weeks between his pay, Kara's income, and the free accommodations at the mattress store.

He waited for a dump truck to pass, then crossed the dirt road and entered a massive warehouse-like structure emblazoned with "Happy Farms."

Inside the building's huge, rustic foyer, a dozen workers in dirty casual clothes walked to and fro. All had CQ scores of 100, which baffled Roger. He peeped into a room. It was a makeshift lunchroom with a refrigerator, chairs, and a few tables. Four workers, all with CQs of 100, were shooting the breeze and scarfing down soft drinks.

Roger noticed restrooms marked "Gents" and "Damsels."

In the foyer, Roger admired a wall painting of a peaceful farm with all sorts of produce, including corn, lettuce, and apple trees. "Happy Farms" was written under the artwork in a rainbow of colors.

Then Roger noticed a set of double doors at the end of a hallway and headed toward them. A sign identified it as the "Processing Department."

He entered and froze. He was aghast and mortified. It was a gigantic room, filled with contraptions and conveyor belts. This was not a happy farm. This was a grisly, synchronized system of torture, misery, and murder. It was a slaughterhouse.

A dozen workers with CQs of 100 were covered in plastic raincoat-like attire and wore safety gloves. They had stoic faces and were slaughtering people strapped to a conveyor belt. The victims were flat on their backs; there were shackles around their wrists and ankles. None had CQ scores.

Several employees were stationed at the beginning of the assembly line; they stunned the helpless humans with bolt guns. Every third person was still conscious—in other words, the bolt gun had failed to work. These folks squirmed and screamed for help. Those who were stunned, as well as those who were fully aware of their predicament, were then advanced to the next phase: the beheading station.

At this stage, a guillotine-like device sliced off their heads. The heads dropped into plastic tubs. The headless bodies then moved forward on the conveyor belt to another team of workers, who hacked off legs and arms with gadgets that resembled chain saws. The limbs, attached via cables to a complicated system of apparatus near the ceiling, were carried off on a different track from the torsos and were ultimately sorted into barrels. In the final step, the bloody stumps were carried out of sight, through a square hole in the wall, which was directly under a sign that read "Skinning."

Roger felt like a ticking bomb. He was certain he would detonate. But he knew it was important to maintain composure and conceal his emotions. He did not want to be exposed as a vate. He stood tall and pretended to be tough and detached from the insanity around him.

He wondered if Keiko was right about the existence of a caste system in which weak people were churned into food. He scanned the room, fearing for his own life. *Will they realize I'm not one of them, strap me to the conveyor belt, and chop off my head? Could my toes end up at the First Street Deli?*

A man named Tanner with a CQ of 100 headed in his direction. Roger gulped hard and darted out of the room, taking refuge in the atrium next to the peaceful farm painting.

Tanner confronted Roger.

"Hey, I've never seen you before. Are you a new processor?"

"Uh… well." Roger stumbled over his words. "I was just checking things out."

"Why would you do that?" Tanner seemed suspicious. "You from the FDA?"

"No. No. No. Marlin from the Big Tractor Store. He sent me."

"Oh, Marlin. Yeah. He's a great guy. Terrific benefits here and if you ask nicely, they'll pay you in cash. Not a lot of places will do that. You starting today?"

"No. No. No... I've got a bad shoulder. Can't do strenuous work."

"Really?" Tanner appeared skeptical. "A bad shoulder. That's a shame."

Tanner wandered to the other side of the room and whispered to Jed, another processor, who wore a toupee and had a CQ of 100.

Roger moved to a window with a sweeping view of the back of the property. An enormous, grassy slope was framed by a thick forest of trees. A private asphalt road ran adjacent to the wooded area.

Roger directed his gaze downward and saw a semi-truck unloading dozens of individuals; none had CQ scores. The people looked frightened, and their clothes were tattered. They were shoved along, single file, by ruthless handlers, all with CQs of 100.

The handlers, who beat the victims with batons when they stepped out of line, forced these poor folks to enter the ground floor of the Happy Farms compound. When the back of the truck was empty, the driver, who had a CQ of 94.6, shut the rear doors and climbed into the vehicle. He drove the semi down the road toward two huge wooden structures in the distance. It seemed like he was going back for another load.

Roger turned to see that in addition to Jed, Tanner was whispering with two other processors: Buck and Floyd, who also had CQ scores of 100. The group was clearly talking about him.

Roger smiled at the men and waved, hoping to assuage their concerns, but they did not reciprocate, so he scooted out the front door, ran to the side of the building, and hid. He peered out, curious as to whether he was being followed.

Lo and behold, he was.

The men exited in search of him. They were accompanied by JP, the manager of the place, who also had a CQ of 100. The group scanned the area but did not see the man they now referred to as "Mr. Bad Shoulder," so they retreated inside the building.

Roger made a beeline for the woodsy area and then ran toward the two structures at the back of the property.

⚘

Roger trekked quite a distance through the woods and came to the first structure, an enormous warehouse. He could see inside because a broken side board left a gap approximately four inches wide.

The structure had trusses, a vaulted ceiling, posts, corbels, stress beams, collar ties, braces, and a roof. There appeared to be hundreds of people stuffed inside; they looked grubby and dejected. To call the conditions primitive would have been an understatement. It was as harsh as harsh can be.

There was feces on the floor. Several people were crying. Flies buzzed. Some individuals tried to swat them away, while others did not expend the effort, probably because they had given up on life.

A few people were sprawled out on wooden platforms without bedding, without pillows. There was a dirt floor, feeding troughs, and watering stations. Some individuals scooped up what looked like cereal and stuffed it into their mouths, while others retrieved water with cupped hands from one of the coffin-sized receptacles. A few people limped as if they had sprains or broken bones, and others had festering wounds.

Roger could not believe his eyes. The whole thing was

surreal. It seemed like Earth had become the most wicked place imaginable. He wondered how the planet could have changed so drastically in just 100 years.

He understood why people had embraced the Luddite lifestyle. Although he considered it strange, at least he could grasp how the public might become suspicious of technology due to hacking, the loss of jobs to robots, the invasion of privacy, and the lack of well-made consumer products—all the things he had read about in the library. A hacker could steal proprietary data, drain bank accounts, and fire off missiles. At least, the popularity of past decades made sense.

But the cruelty at Happy Farms and the First Street Deli was baffling. Roger could not comprehend it. He figured maybe Kara was right when she guessed that God, Allah, Brahma, Buddha, or some other entity had time-traveled the eight to this hellhole of a planet to let them gather information before returning them to 2025.

Kara believed elevator people were special and had a mission: to save society. Roger had no clue how he would make a difference or change the course of history. It seemed improbable that a few vates could convince an entire world to be compassionate and kind.

The partially broken slat allowed Roger to see through to the other side of the warehouse, where there were two uniformed, gun-bearing guards: Kip and Pete. These men patrolled the entryway to the building and had CQs of 100. He also saw a worker inside the warehouse with a CQ of 98.8. This guy held a hose and was spraying water on the walls, ground, and wooden platforms.

While peering at the guards and the worker, something bizarre happened. Roger's eyes became blurry. When his vision cleared, the guards and worker suddenly looked like Nazi officers. Roger blinked hard several times and rubbed his eyes, but he still saw Hermann Goring, Heinrich Himmler, and Joseph Goebbels. It was wacky and unsettling.

Roger wondered if his mind was playing tricks due to the stress of being an outcast and fugitive in an unfamiliar world. Or maybe the hallucination was related to his earlier comment about Nazis at the First Street Deli. Was his brain subconsciously dredging up Hitler imagery? On the other hand, maybe he was going mad. He figured anything was possible in this world that made absolutely no sense.

He remembered as a child experiencing a "hallucination manifestation" or what his mother called a *"man* named *Hal,"* accentuating the first three letters of those two words. Roger sometimes woke up in the middle of the night to go to the bathroom and saw what looked like a bearded and pointy-eared troll standing at the foot of his bed. His mom chalked it up to reading *Three Billy Goats Gruff* before shutting off the lights and settling under the covers. Roger thought his mother's explanation made sense. Hal was a figment of his imagination.

Roger was still looking through the partially broken slat when... the Nazi images suddenly disappeared. The guards and the worker once again looked like themselves.

Guard Kip yelled at the worker, "Get those fucking beasts out of the way so you can hose the place down properly."

"I'm on it." The worker shot water at a group of victims, who screamed and dashed to the other side of the building. Some tumbled to the ground from the intense water pressure.

One of the victims, a young woman with a ponytail, noticed Roger peeking through the hole and inched close to him. "Please help me, mister."

Roger felt sympathy but did not have time to respond, because the worker with the hose moved close to the woman and sprayed her while shouting, "Dumb bitch. Move it."

She screeched and jumped out of the way.

Roger noticed the worker's CQ move up from 98.8 to 98.9. He was surprised to learn that one act of cruelty could affect the score in real-time.

Then something else bad happened. Guard Kip caught a glimpse of Roger peeping through the hole.

Roger quickly ducked, calculating whether he had time to hightail it across the grassy field to the woodsy area without getting caught. He wondered, *Will I be exposed for too long in the open air? Will I get shot while making a run for it? Will I be caught and thrown into prison, or worse, be churned into a meatloaf patty?*

He remained crouched for a mere two seconds before hauling it across the Happy Farms lawn to the wooded area. He sprinted past trees and bushes; he jumped over logs and rocks. He had a burst of energy that only flat-out terror can provide, the kind of stamina that emerges when one is faced with death.

Guard Kip walked around the building to see if there was an intruder but found no one. He chalked it up to the elderly gardener who tended the lawn, thinking this guy had passed the opening while doing his chores. Kip returned to his post and did not report the incident to his boss, JP.

Roger made it to the street in front of Happy Farms. He jogged past parked cars until he reached his truck.

He scanned the area for witnesses, saw no one, slipped into the vehicle, and zoomed away.

Chapter Seven

STEEL BARS AND EMOTIONAL SCARS

Roger drove the mattress store truck down I-85, then passed Boat Lake and took a set of private roads to a parking lot next to a bus pickup zone. He parked and entered the blue-and-white main entrance of the Maryland Zoo. He was there because he had seen a billboard next to the freeway, depicting people behind bars at the site.

He'd realized the article at the library had not been satire. It seemed that people were being used in a number of ways, not just to satisfy culinary desires. Roger was determined to investigate first-hand. He theorized that enslavement, abuse, and killing were sanctioned for all sorts of profit-making purposes in this strange and sordid world.

Inside the zoo, Roger passed an area called Celebration Hill, and then he ventured toward a cluster of displays: all contained imprisoned humans. There was signage that identified each enclosure. There were African pygmies from the Congo next to a cage full of Swedish blonds. The Swedes were lying on their backs, bored, swatting at flies; one was picking at the hair of another.

East Asians inhabited a third cage; one guy was licking his toes. There were Native Americans in another cell: they wore traditional garb and had teepees. Adjacent to them was a wintry, fully glassed-in enclosure that housed Inuit Eskimos, complete with two igloos and a sled. One Eskimo banged her head against the glass, over and over, to convey her melancholy.

An aquatic chamber held synchronized swimmers. Those who were not being forced to perform were huddled in a corner in wet bathing suits, shivering.

There were also cages full of people covered in tattoos, muscle men lifting barbells, and bikini-clad Brazilians jumping from a trampoline through a ring of fire. Not everyone looked "normal," according to societal standards: There were small children with grotesque deformities, people weighing over a thousand pounds, bearded ladies, women with facelifts gone wrong, the most-wrinkled men on the planet, and conjoined twins. There was even a cage titled "Assorted Misfits." These people had abscesses all over their bodies, extra limbs, or burned skin; one guy had an extra ear, which had been transplanted into his arm.

Roger was appalled by the displays but was equally appalled by the zoo visitors, who behaved as if it was a routine day in Baltimore. Some of them had small children. No one seemed bothered by the grief on the victims' faces.

Parents and youngsters smiled, laughed, and arrogantly pointed at the "freaks"—as if to declare their superiority at the expense of others. The caged victims were seen as objects, as something to gawk at, and as inferior to "normal" humans.

They had no value apart from the extent to which they could satisfy the leisure-time whims of the masses.

Roger noticed that no one in a cage seemed remotely content; in fact, many were clearly in mental anguish as they paced hopelessly in circles, bit their skin, or inflicted other types of self-harm. Some even rocked back and forth, a telltale sign of depression and despondency. The zoo was ceaseless misery for the victims—a place full of steel bars and emotional scars.

It reminded Roger of the freak shows he had read about and seen in films, such as *Nightmare Alley.*

In the 1800s, carnivals and traveling circuses exploited those with deformities to produce sensationalist presentations. Spectacles of cruelty were common in those days. Many "abnormal" people were kidnapped, held against their will, and forced to entertain the crowds. Sometimes the directors of these sideshows would inflict pain in order to alter appearance and accentuate peculiarities. Showcasing oddities led to great profits, as it was apparently doing now.

Roger put aside these thoughts. He had seen enough.

He returned to the mattress store truck and left the zoo parking lot. He thought about how Joan would be proud of him. In only a few days, he had become a man of action, a person who no longer conformed to the status quo. This upside-down world had incentivized him to blossom into a person he liked.

Roger had always been disappointed in himself. He'd been a groundhog who never came out of hiding, a bat who never left the solace of his cave. But now he had plans to become a revolutionary, to free the trapped souls destined for the beheading blade and to release the traumatized victims at the zoo. He would not sit around in the comfort of the mattress store, biding his time until Independence Day. It was not in keeping with the man he had become.

While driving, he noticed a business called On the Spot

Butcher Shop. The wording on the storefront read "Fresh! Fresh! Fresh!" He rationalized, *I've been on a fact-finding mission all day, so why stop now?*

Roger parked and entered an unlocked side gate, which led him into a courtyard. He noticed the butcher shop in the front and two auxiliary buildings in the rear. No one seemed to be around. There were discarded tables and chairs in the yard, as well as a food scale, a rusty meat grinder, and some indecipherable metal contraptions.

He entered the first auxiliary building, where he found people crammed into undersized cages. The victims were scrunched up because the enclosures were too small for them to stretch their arms and legs. There were two tiers; some of the cages were piled on top of others. Food, water, urine, and feces fell from the top story onto the people on the lower level. The place was grungy and smelly.

The victims became agitated and fearful when Roger entered; some struggled to move in their cells. Others howled, moaned, or whined. No one had CQ scores.

A preteen girl on the bottom row, who was covered in urine and food debris, stared at Roger and muttered, "Why do you hate me so much? What did I do wrong?"

Roger was emotionally torn and replied, "Nothing. You didn't do anything."

He turned to another girl. "And you. You didn't do anything either."

Then he pointed at captive after captive. "Or you. Or you. Or you. None of you did anything."

Roger wiped tears from his eyes as he bolted back into the courtyard. He peeped around a corner and saw a butcher with a CQ of 100. The man was in the open air, slicing up a dead woman; her blonde hair cascaded off a table.

A second butcher with a CQ of 100, wrapped in a

blood-stained apron, sneaked up behind Roger. "What are you doing here?" he barked.

"Uh… Uh… I was looking for Mr. Potter," Roger tripped over his words. "I was told he works here."

"You were told wrong." The man pointed at the exit.

"Oh, okay. Sorry to have disturbed you."

Roger scampered back to the truck. He figured he had better not do more investigating because he would inevitably find more victims and then feel guilty if he did not have time to rescue them all. Three undercover operations were plenty, especially as he might be working alone. There was no guarantee that the other vates at Paradise Mattress would be willing to help.

During the drive, Roger felt regretful. He wished he had told the poor girl and the other captives in the auxiliary building that he would return for them. He could imagine their fear, their agony, their hopelessness—as well as the cramping involved with being unable to stretch their limbs. Roger was distressed but tried to do his usual compartmentalizing. He needed to stay strong and put a rescue plan in place.

The next stop on the agenda was an office supply store, where Roger bought poster boards, masking tape, notepads, and magic markers. Then he went to a magazine kiosk, where he purchased an assortment of newspapers. He felt it was important to be up on the news about elevator people, and the television in the break room was not a reliable source.

❦

Carl was in front of the mattress store, assuming the role of a human directional. He twirled a cardboard sign like an acrobat, hoping to attract customers. In other words, Bernie was taking his sales job seriously and had designated Carl as the director of advertising. Like everything he did, the old man put muscle, fortitude, and conviction into the task.

Carl prided himself as a jack-of-all-trades and a darn good one at that. He envisioned telling a story one day that began, "Reminds me of the time I was a sign spinner after time-traveling into the future where people were eating people."

Kara came running up the sidewalk. She acknowledged Carl with a nod and rushed into the mattress store, out of breath. She dumped a few hundred dollars on the counter, representing her wages for the day, and then scurried into the break room, where she found Ellen, Bailey, Angus, and Keiko. She plopped into a chair and placed her head in her hands.

"I don't know what to do. I don't want to go back, but I promised. I don't know what to do."

Bernie entered, wearing a smile. "Sold two mattresses today. I'm definitely employee of the month." He noticed the sour mood in the room. "Hey, what's going on?"

❧

It was the following morning in the mattress store break room. The vates had stumbled upon several vintage games in a closet, including Hasbro's Twister. This was essentially a plastic floor mat with large blue, green, yellow, and red circles; there was also a dial that instructed players where to place their hands and feet. It had become a fad from the 1960s through the 1980s, following the same popularity as another novelty item: the hula hoop. Twister had been controversial; some people called it "sex in a box" due to the physical closeness required during play.

Angus, Bailey, Keiko, and Bernie were laughing and contorting themselves into pretzels in accordance with Twister's rules. Ellen and Carl were the "spinners." Kara, who was dressed in business attire, watched the fun.

"What does this remind you of, Carl?" Keiko asked.

"Not a thing." Carl grinned.

"Maybe it reminds you of the time you discovered America with Christopher Columbus?" Keiko offered.

Everyone laughed.

"Nope." Carl chuckled.

"Maybe it reminds you of the time you flew to the moon in Apollo 13?" Bailey said.

"Nope." Carl smiled.

"We're just joking around, Carl," Bernie added.

"I know. You aren't the first skeptic who's crossed my storied path."

"We just want a juicy story," Kara said. "What about all these circles and primary colors. It must remind you of something."

"Well… there was the time I won the Straightest Tie Contest at the Piccadilly Fair."

"Tell us more." Kara grinned.

"It was 1985, and I was wearing my yellow necktie. It had red trim and blue polka dots. I won a stuffed penguin, and I gave it to my nephew."

"That's more like it," Kara said. "That's the Carl we know and love."

Everyone, including Carl, laughed.

On the other side of the room. Roger was constructing a makeshift conference facility. Blank poster boards were taped to the wall. Notepads, pens, magic markers, and a stack of newspapers rested on an oblong table. Roger carefully positioned eight straight-bank chairs: one for each vate. He had everything arranged for a meeting. The seven abandoned the Twister game and headed over.

"We've got our situation room," Roger announced.

"That's good," Kara replied. "Cause we definitely have a situation."

"Did you know the cruelty quotient can change from one second to the next?" Roger asked.

"Everyone at Worthington's already 100, the level of satanic. It's the new 666. I wonder what my number is. Are you sure I don't have one?" Kara stared at her friends, who shook their heads.

"I don't think vates get numbers," Roger replied.

"It's funny how they call us vates." Kara slipped on her jacket. "They think it's an insult, but the word comes from old Celtic. It means prophet or soothsayer."

"The homeless dude was right," Bernie said. "We are the chosen."

"Chosen to get stuck in a freezer with a hundred dead bodies," Angus added.

"Chosen to go AWOL from responsibility." Bailey suddenly became emotional and ran out of the room.

"Bailey, where are you going?" Kara shouted.

The seven heard the door to the street slam shut, indicating Bailey had left the building.

"She's probably taking a walk," Ellen stated. "It clears her head."

Roger examined a newspaper. "It says 362,000 people disappeared when we did, but there are only 10,000 cities on the planet. That means there might be another twenty-eight elevator people right here in Baltimore."

"362,000? That's a hell of a lot of folks," Carl added.

"One person out of every 22,000 is an elevator person." Kara did the calculation in her head.

"We should search for them," Ellen said. "Maybe they can tell us how the government decides which people are slaves."

"I doubt they know anything more than we do." Roger perused a second newspaper.

"Plus, how would we track them down?" Kara grabbed a

bagel. "I'd better hurry. See you tonight." She raised her fist. "Go Team Terrorist."

She left.

❧

Half an hour later, Ellen, Carl, and Roger sat in the makeshift situation room while Bernie inventoried mattresses. Angus and Keiko watched a basketball game on television. Although there was a significant amount of TV snow and irritating horizontal lines, the sound was clear.

Roger drew a map of the Worthington Research Institute on a poster board.

"You folks want stories? I got a doozy about maps," Carl offered.

"Give it to us, Carl…. Wait… let me sit down," Ellen said playfully as she sat and braced herself for something outrageous.

"There was the time Jacques Cousteau and I drew a diagram of the Strait of Malacca. We were searching for a sunken treasure. Finally found it, but we had to fight off pirates. Worth twenty-two million."

Roger and Ellen stared at Carl, as if this tale was a little too tall.

"What happened to the money?" Roger asked.

"A whale ate it."

"Of course," Roger replied sarcastically.

"I think your nose is a tad longer than it was five minutes ago." Ellen laughed.

Roger directed his friends back to the work at hand, pointing at the map. "Okay, this is the building, and this is the alley."

A player on television missed a basket, and Keiko groaned. "Oh, come on."

"Looks like you're gonna owe me some cash, little bro." Angus laughed.

Ellen spoke to Angus and Keiko. "You boys need to get over here and help."

"We're gonna sit out the two weeks," Keiko said.

"Excuse me?" Ellen looked pissed off.

"We don't want to get involved," Angus added.

"Hey, we saved your ass, you lazy Mother Teresa." Ellen put her hands on her hips. "This is important to Kara and Roger, so you damn well better get over here."

"You'd be Angus Primavera right now." Carl chuckled.

"Angus with pickles on rye," Bernie chimed in.

"Hey, you two. On the double." Ellen made a loud whistling sound by putting her fingers to her lips. She pointed at two chairs.

Angus and Keiko rolled their eyes and dragged themselves to the table.

"I can't believe Bailey's not back," Roger said.

⁘

After leaving the mattress store, Kara waited in the shadows outside a hair salon that was directly across the street from the Worthington Research Institute. She planned to do the groundwork for that night's operation.

Roger had agreed to help her rescue the victims at the lab. Later in the week, they would save those at Happy Farms, the butcher shop, and the zoo. She was delighted that she and Roger were on the same page: they had embraced their "inner terrorist."

Ellen and Carl had also offered to help, but she was unsure about Bernie, Angus, Keiko, and Bailey. She hoped they'd join the effort, especially as she figured at least six people were necessary to pull off each mission.

Not only would Kara need to be sneaky that morning, but she knew she would somehow have to make it through the day, sequestering herself in the filing room while ignoring any sobs, shrieks, and pleas that might come from the next room. It would be hard; it broke her heart to hear the victims' cries of distress. Kara had to finish the day because remuneration was crucial for covering food costs. No one else had any financial prospects. She needed to accumulate as much money as possible until another form of employment could be secured.

Kara waited and waited. Finally, she saw Olive approaching the front entrance of Worthington and hurried to her.

"Hey, Olive. Wait up."

"You're an hour early."

"Want to get a head start. Lots of filing to be done."

Olive unlocked the entry door while Kara zeroed in on the key.

They entered the establishment, and Olive placed the key in a desk drawer in the reception area before heading back to the lab.

Kara furtively removed the key, stuck it in her pocket, and yelled, "Olive, I think I left the stove on at home. I'll be back in fifteen minutes."

"Okay," Olive hollered back.

Kara rushed out of the building and went to a locksmith, who made a copy of the key. Then she returned to Worthington, but unfortunately, she found Olive sitting at the desk in the reception area; she prayed her associate had not checked the drawer.

"Want some coffee?" Kara asked.

"No, thanks."

Kara retreated to a tiny kitchen off the laboratory. She poured a cup of decaf and then intentionally dropped it on the floor. The mug broke into a dozen pieces, and hot liquid splashed everywhere: on the cabinetry, fridge, and walls.

"Aaaaah! Help! Olive!" Kara screamed.

Olive dashed into the room.

"I'm sorry." Kara pretended to be ill. "I'm feeling really dizzy. I need to sit down. Could you clean it up for me? I'm so sorry."

Olive seemed annoyed. "I'll take care of it."

Kara made her way to the reception area and slipped the key back into the drawer. Then she sat in a chair, pretending to be lightheaded.

Olive entered. "I hope you can work today because it's just you, me, and Dr. Dijon. The others are off until tomorrow."

"I'll be fine."

Several hours later, Kara was in the filing room when she happened upon a folder titled "Relevance of Research Data." She examined the contents and found every experiment officially stamped with the phrase, "Test results: Worthless. Does not extrapolate." Kara was mortified that Worthington employees were not only torturing victims but doing it unnecessarily.

She studied the folder more closely, relying on her medical background. It was clear that the results of every test conducted at Worthington had been determined to lack value. They were superficial; they had no more significance than a study on who could twiddle their thumbs the fastest. Kara was quite sure the monsters—who called themselves researchers—mutilated and murdered victims for one reason: money. It was all about lining their pockets with funds from research grants. It was the only logical explanation.

Kara stumbled upon another folder. It was titled "Research Subject Breeding Centers." Inside, she found a list of businesses that supplied the "specimens" to Worthington Research. There were four: Willis Specimens, Premiere Research Aids, Toskins-Wright, and Living Solutions, Inc.

She peeped through the window in the door to make sure no one was nearby, folded up the document, and stuffed it into her pocket.

Seconds later, Dr. Dijon entered. "Dr. Carson, I'd like you to conduct a toxicity test. Olive will explain what you need to do."

"But this is only my second day." Kara was desperate to wiggle out of the assignment. "Don't you want me to finish the filing?"

"The client needs results, and I don't have enough staff. Come along."

Kara begrudgingly followed Dr. Dijon into the lab. Olive stood next to a pump, feeding tubes, and beakers filled with thick gray liquid.

Dr. Dijon told Olive, "Please explain the procedure to Dr. Carson."

Then she left the room.

Olive said, "You'll use the specimens in cage two."

Kara glanced at the victims in the second enclosure. She saw what appeared to be girls and boys between the ages of eight and ten.

"You'll insert the feeding tube into the mouth and down the throat of each subject," Olive said. "Then you'll take the drain cleaning product—that's what we're testing—and pump it into each tube. You'll begin with a tablespoon, then increase it to half a cup, then one cup, then two cups. You'll note when half the specimens are dead. If they all die, no big deal. But take copious notes."

"Do you ever feel bad for them?" Kara asked.

"What? No. Of course not. They're inferior. They were put on Earth for our benefit."

"Why do you think that?"

"Everybody thinks that. The question is… why don't you think that? They're not as smart as we are, and frankly I don't even think they feel pain in the same way."

"What about their screams?"

"That's just reflex or instinct. Hey, don't let Dr. Dijon hear you talking like this, or she'll put you in a cage." Olive laughed.

Suddenly, Kara's eyes went all wonky. They seemed to be playing tricks on her. Her vision became blurry, but when it cleared, Olive looked like Cambodia's Pol Pot of the Khmer Rouge. He was wearing a uniform and a military hat.

Kara blinked hard, rubbed her eyes, and tried to shake herself away from what she assumed was a delusion. Then pronto, Olive looked like herself again. Kara did not know what to make of what had happened and thought it best not to mention it to anyone at the lab.

Olive continued with the instructions. "If they scream or convulse too much, you can use these—the blue ones—to sedate them. It knocks them out instantly and keeps them asleep for hours."

Olive presented Kara with six blue single-dose syringes. Kara placed them in her pocket.

"If the specimens really get on your nerves, you can use the black ones to euthanize them," Olive explained. "Just make sure they're close to death and take lots of notes before you give them the needle."

Olive furnished six black single-dose syringes.

Kara dumped them into her pocket with the others. Olive looked at the clock.

"Eek, it's eleven. You can start after lunch. I'm gonna grab a bite at the Chinese. You want to come?"

"No. Thanks."

"You're missing the best oxtail soup in town."

Olive grabbed her purse and left.

Kara paced the lab in a quandary.

Tick, tock, tick, tock.

She glanced at the clock, paced some more, checked the time again, and continued walking in circles. Finally, she stopped, stared at the incinerator, plucked a black syringe from her pocket, and opened cage number two.

"Okay." She motioned at the specimens. "Everyone out. Hurry up."

The victims emerged from the enclosure and stared at her, terrified.

Kara returned the syringe to her pocket and hurried over to the back door and opened it. Again, there was no alarm.

"Okay. Chop-chop. No time to dillydally."

The victims seemed puzzled and were motionless, so Kara shoved them out the door and into the alley. "Get as far away from here as you can," she hollered, but some children stood there, frozen.

Kara pretended to be a monster. She lifted her arms high in the air and growled. "Aaaaah, Aaaaah. Go. Go. Hurry up."

With that, the victims became scared and started running. Kara shut the back door.

Other captives cried out, "Help," "Please," and "I want to go, too."

"It won't be long. Just a few more hours. I promise." She tried to reassure them, but they did not seem to comprehend her words.

Kara felt pressure. She was under a time crunch. She had to act before noon, to get her con game in place. She went to the incinerator, scooped up ashes, and dumped them onto a large tray. Then she took some of the bones and teeth from the bottom of the furnace-like contraption, which were left over from previous burnings, and situated them next to the ashes. The clock read 11:30.

Kara poured some of the thick drain-cleaning solution from the beakers into the bottom of a trash can and covered the substance with paper and other garbage. Then she wrote in a notebook at breakneck speed, completing page after page of nonsense, which she hoped would pass as scientific data.

At 12:05, when Olive and Dr. Dijon returned from lunch, Kara pretended to be burning the final specimen in the incinerator.

"I was able to get the experiment completed during lunch. Unfortunately, all the specimens died. But I made detailed notes." Kara acted upbeat.

Dr. Dijon was clearly skeptical. She extracted the tray from the incinerator and noticed the pile of ash, teeth, and bones, which did indeed resemble the remains of a body.

"Let me see." Dr. Dijon held out her hand, motioning that she wanted to review Kara's report.

Kara passed over the notebook.

Dr. Dijon reviewed the first page, the second, and the third.

"This isn't sufficient," Dr. Dijon said matter-of-factly. "You'll need to redo the experiment. You can use the specimens in cage five."

Kara looked at the eight young women behind steel bars in cage five. She felt cornered and frantic, although she did not outwardly show it.

There was only one thing left to do: fake illness. Kara once again pretended to be faint. She fell into a metal cart, which rolled into the wall with a thud. Then she drooped herself over it like a rag doll, head down.

"I'm sorry," Kara mumbled. "I'm really dizzy."

"She's been dizzy all day," Olive added.

"Do you think I could go home early and do the experiment first thing in the morning?" Kara asked.

Dr. Dijon sighed. "You won't be paid for the second half of the day."

"That's fine. I just need to go home."

Kara received her half-day pay and hobbled out of the lab, still posing as an invalid. She did not pay much attention, but she passed a handyman as she headed down the sidewalk.

The man entered Worthington Research and spoke to Dr. Dijon and Olive.

"I'm here to fix an alarm."

Chapter Eight

SMASH AND GRAB

The situation room in the mattress store was fully operational. A poster board affixed to the wall listed the proposed rescue missions and the order in which they would take place: 1) Worthington Research Institute, 2) On the Spot Butcher Shop, 3) Willis Specimens, 4) Premiere Research Aids, 5) Toskins-Wright, 6) Living Solutions, Inc., 7) Happy Farms, and 8) The Maryland Zoo.

Other poster boards showed diagrams of these locations and an inventory of items needed for each operation, such as a flashlight, gloves, one or two trucks, and dark clothing.

Sprawled out on the oblong table were pens, maps of the city, newspaper clippings, and notepads filled with extensive writing. It was afternoon, and Roger sat at the table, studying a map, while Ellen and Kara looked over his shoulder. Angus and Keiko played a card game on the other side of the room.

"I still think we should let them out over here near the homeless shelter." Ellen pointed at a location on the map.

"No," Roger replied. "We've already decided they'll be better off in the suburbs. Less chance the genocidal maniacs will track them down."

"Speaking of genocide," Kara said, "I had a weird thing happen today. I don't know if it has anything to do with going blind in the elevator, but my vision got all cockeyed for a few seconds. One of the researchers looked like Pol Pot."

"Who's that?" Keiko walked over and joined the conversation.

"He was a Cambodian dictator. He killed two million people," Kara said.

"I had something like that happen yesterday," Roger added. "The guards at Happy Farms turned into Nazi officers. Then they turned back. It was just a hallucination."

"I believe in reincarnation," Ellen said. "Maybe they *really were* Nazis and that Cambodian guy. Maybe they've come back to life in new bodies and only vates can see them."

"Or maybe we're going insane," Kara interjected.

"We could be in an asylum and just not know it," Keiko suggested.

"My mustard lady boss is a lot like Nurse Ratched." Kara laughed.

"My third husband was in the loony bin," Ellen offered.

"Frederico?" Kara questioned.

"No," Ellen replied. "Frederico was crabby, not crazy."

"How many husbands have you had?" Kara asked.

"Only three. Not counting the first two. The first two aren't worth counting."

Carl and Bernie hurried through the door.

"We searched the park," Bernie said. "And the streets. We couldn't find her."

"My lord, I hope she wasn't picked up by the cops." Ellen looked worried.

"I'm sure she's fine," Kara added.

"We'll look for her tonight after we finish the mission," Roger said.

"This is so exciting." Ellen grinned. "We're gonna be outlaws."

❧

The elevator people (minus Bailey) had engaged in a serious conversation about going rogue.

Kara and Roger were all in. They had seen victims up close and had, in some cases, made promises to assist. They could not shrug off the cruelty and live with themselves. They could not pretend they hadn't seen beheading machines, Draize tests, rows of hanging corpses, dinner plates of ears, cans of pickled feet, and victims crammed into tiny cages unable to spread their limbs.

They figured vates around the world had been reacting to this freakish society, fighting against the morals, mores, and laws of 2125. And they were being punished for their rebellion, for resistance, and for liberating the oppressed. This was surely the reason they were being detained, thrown in jail, or, in some cases, shot. The newspapers reported relatively high numbers of captured and killed elevator people but, oddly enough, never explored the motives behind their actions. Vates were simply described as "extremist," "mentally unstable," "evil," or "alien." It was clear that the general public condoned these simplistic and fallacious labels.

Kara had once taken a psychology course titled "The

Systems and Dynamics of Oppression" and had learned why liberation never sits well with exploiters.

"Abusers like to abuse. That's how they accumulate wealth and feel superior," Kara said. "Prejudice against those deemed inferior makes those in power feel better about their own sad and compassionless lives. It's not just butchers, researchers… hands-on killers. The public's complicit. Indirectly, they're exploiting as well. They know it deep down. Rather than look in the mirror, they prefer to label people like us as 'kooks' and 'bogeymen.'"

"So, you're saying this is gonna be an uphill battle for us kooks?" Roger chuckled.

"We're climbing Mount Everest in flip-flops," Kara replied. "But it doesn't mean we can't get to the top and plant a victory flag."

Next, the vates discussed the risk of getting caught. Kara believed the job at Worthington Research would be easy because she had a key to the front door and the alarm on the back door was faulty. She had no idea it had been repaired and would prove to be a factor that could unravel the operation.

Comradery and peer pressure played into deciding whether to participate in the missions. In other words, some of the vates felt coerced by their friends.

Kara knew all about the Solomon Asch conformity studies, in which it was found that a majority of people will go along with the crowd even when they have reservations or know the crowd is wrong. She also knew about the Stanley Milgram experiments that essentially proved the same thing.

There was a bit of this join-the-bandwagon, lend-a-helping-hand, give-and-take swirling around, especially concerning Bernie. He was influenced to follow others. But this was not the only reason Carl, Ellen, Keiko, and Angus agreed to participate. They had additional reasons for deciding to morph into rebels and violate the law.

Carl was Mr. Adventure. He was game for anything, and the wilder, the better. He'd never committed a crime and figured it was about time he found out what all the fuss was about. It might be a new adrenaline rush, a height he had never known. He was readier than ready could be.

Ellen had been born with a bit of daredevil fairy dust, although she'd always kept her nonconformity under wraps. A passion bubbled deep inside, and she craved to unleash it. She wondered if life could be more fulfilling if she ceased to be a rubber stamp, if she stopped assuming the role of Ms. Obedient. Since she was no longer married, she felt free to explore her essence and craft her own unique values and ideals. She thought an uprising against 2125 was the perfect place to start.

Keiko and Angus did not want to go to Worthington Research, or participate in any of the missions, but felt railroaded due to reciprocation or what might be called you-scratch-my-back-and-I'll-scratch-yours.

Angus had faced death, or at least imprisonment, at the First Street Deli, and the others had come to his aid. They did not have to help. They could have written him off as a casualty of time travel. Instead, Roger and Kara risked their freedom, and possibly their lives, to help a guy who had not been all that nice to them. Angus was willing to concede that he could be a rotter at times. Anyway, it had been settled. Angus, Kara, Roger, Ellen, Carl, Bernie, and Keiko had agreed to engage in the furtive operations—or at least see how the first one went and take it from there.

∾

It was dark outside and an hour before curfew. Carl parked the mattress store truck next to the emergency exit at Worthington Research, and all the vates (except Bailey) climbed out. The plan was to open the back door of the business from the inside, lead the victims into the rear of the vehicle, and transport them to suburbia where, hopefully, kind strangers would come to their aid.

"You two be ready," Roger said to Angus and Carl, who were tasked with watching the truck.

"Aye, aye, captain." Carl gave a salute and clicked his heels.

Angus rolled his eyes.

Roger, Kara, Bernie, Keiko, and Ellen went to the front of the building, carrying flashlights and knapsacks. Kara used her key to open the door.

"That was pretty darn easy." Ellen smiled.

"Let's start the demolition." Bernie headed into the laboratory with Ellen and Keiko.

Roger started to follow, but Kara noticed a safe under the reception desk. It had a tiny sticker attached, bearing what looked like a three-digit combination.

"Hey, there's a safe, and it looks like a combination," she shouted. "Maybe I should try to open it."

"No." Roger flashed a disapproving look. "We're not common thieves."

Then he joined the others in the lab.

Kara heard banging and smashing in the other room, as well as Bernie's howls of delight. She glanced around to make sure she was alone and tried the combination. To her surprise, the safe opened. To her even greater surprise, there were stacks of money inside, mostly 20-dollar and 100-dollar bills.

She was in a quandary. She hemmed and hawed over whether she should yield to Roger or steal the loot. She reasoned that theft might be wise because it would make it seem like petty hoodlums had broken into the facility. If the cops thought freeing victims was the purpose of the break-in, they would assume the culprits were vates.

Kara emptied her knapsack, placing a crowbar, hammer,

saw, and gloves on the floor. Then she removed the money from the vault, checking again to make sure she was alone. She loaded her knapsack with the cash, but then noticed a desk drawer; it was ajar. She opened it farther to find a revolver, which she also crammed into her knapsack.

"Wow, Colonel Mustard's a whole lot dumber than she looks," she mumbled.

Kara joined the others in the laboratory.

Ellen slammed a sledgehammer onto a cart full of funnels and beakers. The glassware crashed to the floor.

"Great for stress reduction. Better than chamomile and a warm bath." Ellen appeared joyful as she ripped the scarf from her head and threw it on the ground. She shook out her hair, surprising everyone that it was so long. It came down to her waist, which was unusual for a woman of her advanced age.

Keiko opened the incinerator door and screamed in horror. There was a dead man on a tray; he had no eyes or ears. "Nasty!" He backed away.

Roger shut the incinerator door and flipped the "on" switch, while Ellen knocked over a shelf full of products primed to be tested: Best Oven Cleaner, Grantley Paint, and Sludge-Free Clog Remover. They fell to the ground.

The Grantley product opened, and purple paint spilled all over the place.

The caged victims seemed afraid of the demolition activity.

One asked, "What are you doing?"

Another muttered, "Please don't hurt me."

"We're not gonna hurt you." Kara approached the cages. "We have to destroy the lab. Otherwise, they'll just replace you."

The victims did not seem to understand; some cocked their heads, confused.

Roger opened the incinerator door to find the corpse was

now ash, bones, and teeth. He and Keiko piled a bunch of lab torture devices, including the Draize test braces, onto the tray. Then Roger turned on the incinerator again.

"Are you sure there's no alarm?" Bernie pointed at the emergency exit.

"Yeah," Kara replied. "It doesn't work."

The vates unlocked cage after cage. Victims came out. Some were tentative, whereas others embraced their freedom.

Bernie opened the back door, and the alarm sounded. The noise blared like an ambulance siren.

"That's weird. It wasn't working this morning." Kara was bewildered.

Now panicked by the nonstop ringing, the vates quickly ushered the victims through the exit.

"Let's go," Roger said.

"Come on. Out the door," Kara added.

Carl and Angus helped shove the people into the back of the truck. Two of them squeezed around the vehicle and sprinted down the alley.

"Those two rascals are making a run for it." Carl pointed.

"Well, at least we got them out," Ellen replied.

It appeared that everyone was out of the building, so Angus closed the back doors of the truck.

Carl climbed into the driver's seat. Ellen, Angus, and Keiko scrunched up next to him on the passenger side of the cabin. There was no room for Roger, Kara, or Bernie.

"What about you, boss?" Carl asked.

"Just get out of here," Roger said. "We'll find our way back."

The mattress store truck zoomed away.

Roger, Kara, and Bernie reentered the lab, where they saw a dark-haired little girl cowering in the corner with purple paint all over her hair, skin, and clothes.

"Oh, my gosh," Kara exclaimed. "We forgot one."

"I'll grab her." Roger lifted her and rushed into the reception area but saw the flashing lights of a squad car through the storefront blinds.

"Out the back," he said.

Everyone dashed out the rear.

"Where's my mommy?" the little girl asked.

Roger, still carrying the child, made tracks down the alley with Bernie at his side. Kara was far behind; her shoe had gotten caught in a drain grate. Roger started to circle back, but she waved him away.

"Go. Go. Just go."

Kara freed her shoe just as she noticed a cop car in the distance, heading in her direction. She climbed into a dumpster so as not to be seen and pulled the gun from her knapsack while peeping through the opening between the bin and the rubber lid.

The black and white whizzed right past the dumpster in pursuit of Roger, Bernie, and the little girl.

Roger, Bernie, and the child scurried down a walkway that was too narrow for the police cruiser.

Officer Lucy, who had a CQ of 98.7, slammed on the brakes, jumped out of her vehicle, and fired shots at the vates, but missed. She cursed, slid back into the driver's seat of the squad car, and hit the gas.

Officer Juan was on the passenger side. He was twenty years old, had a CQ of 95.2, and was the other half of the two-person law enforcement unit. Although Juan was a newcomer to the force, he was baffled by his partner's actions.

"Is it protocol to shoot them?" he asked.

"They're just filthy vates." Lucy scowled.

"Copy that." Juan smirked and did an evil hand rub, as if he'd watched too many villains in vintage cartoons. "We got a date with a dead vate."

"I know where they're going." Lucy made a right turn.

Bernie and Roger, who was carrying the girl, veered down a walkway between two buildings. The squad car appeared one hundred yards behind them and slammed to a stop.

Cops Lucy and Juan jumped out and fired their guns but missed.

The chase continued. The cops popped back into their vehicle, hoping to cut the vates off at the next street.

Roger, Bernie, and the little girl reached a softball field, where there were two dugouts and a storage shed.

Suddenly Roger's vision went askew, just as it had at Happy Farms.

And poof… the little girl resembled a black kitten. She was covered in purple paint and said, "I want my mommy. Where's my mommy?"

Roger was taken aback as she wiggled out of his arms and leaped to the grass.

"I need to find my mommy."

Roger rubbed his eyes and shook his head. *This hallucination seems so darn real. Why do I keep seeing a man named Hal?*

"Let's hide in the shed," Bernie yelled.

Roger shifted his attention back to the escape and broke the lock on the shed door with a hammer from his knapsack.

The black kitten hightailed it across the softball field and disappeared into the woods.

By this time, Cop Lucy had tracked down the vates. She hid behind signage at an apartment building and secretly peered at Bernie and Roger as they entered the storage shed.

She spoke into her walkie-talkie. "Two vates at the Miller softball field. We've got them cornered."

Inside the shed were bats, mitts, and other softball equipment. Roger and Bernie squatted, garnishing bats as weapons.

They figured the gig was up if the police were able to uncover their hiding spot.

✑

Kara climbed out of the dumpster and noticed two cop cars heading in her direction, one from each end of the alley. She was trapped, so she bolted into Worthington Research and locked the back door.

She ran to the reception area and peered through the blinds to find two officers—Stan and Larry—standing next to their squad car. Kara recognized them as the same cops from the First Street Deli.

Stan and Larry had been told by headquarters to "hold tight" until Detective Ponderosa arrived.

Kara returned to the lab and peeped out the back window. She saw a contingent of cops. These officers were approaching the rear entrance of the building, so she put a straight chair under the doorknob for fortification.

She paced and paced, brainstorming how to finagle herself out of the seemingly impossible predicament.

Finally, she came up with an idea. She grabbed Ellen's scarf from the floor and wrapped it around her nose and mouth like a bandit. She checked her gun. It was not loaded, so she searched for bullets in the reception area drawers. She came up empty.

"No bullets? Really?" she mumbled. "Colonel Mustard needs a candlestick upside the head."

Then she burst out the front entrance of Worthington with her empty gun pointed at Stan and Larry. "Get your hands up, or I'll blow your heads off."

Frightened, they raised their arms.

"Now turn around and face the building," Kara ordered. "And no funny business. Against the wall."

They did as they were told.

Kara got into their squad car. Like before, she found the key under the mat on the driver's side. She started the engine and sped away.

Larry and Stan turned around, befuddled.

"Not again," Stan mumbled.

"Why do you keep leaving the key under the mat?" Larry shook his head.

Kara explored street after street, trying to figure out where Roger and Bernie might be.

A voice reverberated over the police radio. "Calling all available units. Two vates at the Miller softball field in the storage shed."

Kara grabbed the radio's microphone. "Car 38. We've got it covered."

The dispatcher's voice shot back, "Who's this?"

"It's wa, wa, wa, wa, wa, wa." Kara tried to sound incomprehensible.

"Car 38. I think we have a bad connection. Back at me."

Kara threw down the microphone and veered toward the softball field.

Bernie and Roger were sitting on the ground inside the shed, still clutching baseball bats, when they heard Cop Lucy's voice. She was using a megaphone.

"We know you're in there. Come out with your hands on your head."

"Shit," Roger said.

"You think they'll kill us or throw us in jail?" Bernie asked.

"I don't know, but either way, July fourth is rained out."

"On the bright side, I never thought I'd make it to the next century," Bernie replied.

"It's been nice doing time travel with you," Roger said.

"Same here."

At that moment, Kara arrived at the softball field in the

black and white. She saw cops Lucy and Juan, but her vision got fuzzy, and… suddenly, they looked like Jason from *Friday the 13th*. They wore menacing hockey masks. They stood next to the dugout, blocking the path to the shed. Kara barreled toward them.

"Move," she mumbled. "Move. Move. Out of the way."

The masked "Jasons" dove into the dugout in the nick of time.

Kara jammed on the brakes in front of the shed.

Inside, Bernie and Roger were discussing the agony of defeat.

"I think this is our *Butch Cassidy and the Sundance Kid* moment," Roger said. "Let's go."

The two men came running out of the shed, screaming at the top of their lungs, only to find Kara in the police car.

"Kara?" Roger said. "It's Kara."

The two men jumped into the vehicle, while Lucy and Juan, who still looked like hockey goalies, pulled themselves out of the dugout, dirty and disheveled. They watched the squad car speed away and fired in its direction.

Roger and Bernie peered out the back window to see two freaks in hockey masks, shooting at their car.

⤜

An hour later, at the Worthington Research Institute, Detective Julie Ponderosa met with Dr. Dijon and officers Lucy and Juan. She took a report while other cops sifted through debris, searching for clues.

"They not only destroyed the lab and stole the specimens," Dr. Dijon complained, "they broke into my safe."

Detective Ponderosa asked, "Have you hired any new employees lately?"

Chapter Nine

HELL'S BELLS! THEY'RE BACK AT THE ZELLES

It was past curfew. The gang had just completed the undercover operation at the Worthington Research Institute, which had almost spiraled out of control. Everyone was safe, munching on potato chips and drinking apple cider in the mattress store back room, except for Bailey, who was still missing. Roger and Bernie were grateful to Kara; she had once again saved the day.

"That was a hoot." Ellen smiled.

"Some might call it jollification." Carl chuckled.

"Yeah, well you two were in a cushy truck while we were being chased by freaks in hockey masks," Bernie replied.

"You saw the masks, too?" Kara said.

"So did I," Roger interjected.

"They looked like Jason from *Friday the 13th*," Kara added.

"What about the kitten?" Roger asked.

"Yeah. The black-and-purple cat." Bernie grabbed another chip.

"Why would we be having the same hallucination?" Roger wondered.

"Seems like Ellen might be spot-on about reincarnation," Carl said. "Maybe they're real people who have come back to life."

"No," Kara replied. "*Friday the 13th* is fiction. It's not based on a true story. I think the person who brought us here is manipulating us to see things. But why? If we could figure it out… it could be the key to the whole thing."

"It might be a riddle," Roger offered. "We could be trapped in some sort of worldwide escape room."

"Yeah. Maybe we need to piece together clues." Kara knew that only 15 percent of the public are able to free themselves from escape rooms, or at least that was what her father had told her back in 2015. He had been a puzzles and detective games enthusiast. It was a hobby for him. Plus, he used to drag her to murder mystery parties and scavenger hunts; they would try to defeat the other contestants. They prevailed an impressive 49 percent of the time.

Next, the vates explored whether there were any links between Pol Pot, Jason, black cats, and Nazis. All, except the feline, represented mass killers. This was, of course, compatible with the high CQ scores of the butchers and assassins who had become the focus of the vision shifts. On the other hand, the black cat was baffling. No one could see a connection, so Kara plunged into a brief history lesson about the symbolism and superstition related to this domesticated creature. She hoped to touch on something that might be a catalyst for a promising theory.

"There's obviously a myth in the U.S. that black cats bring bad luck," Kara said.

"Then this makes *no* sense," Roger replied sarcastically. "None of us could ever have bad luck."

Everyone laughed.

"In earlier centuries, black cats were believed to be witches in disguise," Kara continued. "They were killed during the Inquisition and Salem witch trials."

"That's horrible," Ellen exclaimed. "Those poor creatures."

"However, in the United Kingdom, a black cat means good luck," Kara added. "In Japan they're seen as a blessing, and in ancient Egypt, they were perceived as divine. So, it runs the gamut."

"I had a divine feline," Carl said. "The Great Catsby. She sat next to my computer, staring at the mouse. She was in love with that little plastic mouse."

"Got to hand it to you, Carl." Ellen laughed. "You've got a story for every occasion. You're always the belle of the ball."

"Glad you appreciate my glass slippers, ma'am." He took a bow.

"We all like your glass slippers, Carl," Kara joked. "Even when they're not a perfect fit."

The vates chuckled.

"Well… if this is an escape room or puzzle, I don't think we have enough pieces to venture a guess." Roger took a swig of cider.

"Keiko and I don't want to help anymore," Angus said. "We just want to chill until the fourth."

"This could be a test," Kara guessed. "By saving lives, maybe we're guaranteeing our return to 2025."

"That washes with me." Carl saluted Kara. "I'm game for another assignment, chief."

Kara looked at Angus. "If you and Keiko don't want to help

anymore, you'll probably just get stuck here forever. But it's your choice."

Angus sighed and stared at her for a beat. "Okay. Fine. We'll *think* about it."

"Guys, we need to find Bailey." Kara inspected a map on the table. "I bet I know where she is."

✑

Roger and Kara went to the Zelles Hotel. They figured it was the only place Bailey could be, unless she had been hauled off by the police or killed. She was desperate to return to 2025, so it made sense that she would see the hotel as a portal. It was her only connection with the past. The hotel was the most promising conduit for getting back to her baby daughter.

Kara peered through the glass at the front of the building and then tugged on the locked doors.

She and Roger circled the edifice in search of a way inside. They eventually came upon a smashed window. The glass had been broken by loose bricks; a half dozen lay on the floor just inside the opening. They figured it was how Bailey had entered.

They climbed through the hole and found themselves in a dark corridor.

They were surrounded by eerie blackness. They could see only the areas illuminated by their flashlights. The ambiance reminded them of a horror movie, as did the yellowed rose-bouquet wallpaper and the chipped, vintage wall sconces.

They crept down the hallway, trying doors, but every room was locked tighter than a casket.

"Bailey?" Kara yelled. "Bailey?"

"Bailey?" Roger chimed in. "Where are you?"

They came to the lobby, which had the same Victorian furnishings and signs that read "Under Construction." The "Out of Order" placard above the elevator was still there.

Roger pushed the call button several times.

"I wonder if she went back to 2025," Kara said.

They waited and waited, but nothing happened. The elevator never came.

"The stairs are over there." Roger pointed. "Let's check the other floors. You take two. I'll take three and meet you on four."

Kara made it to the second floor and wandered down the dark hall, tugging on locked doors and yelling for Bailey.

There was no answer.

Suddenly, she was jumped from behind by Cop Lucy, who had been hiding in an alcove. She and her partner, Juan, had been ordered to inspect the hotel for elevator people.

After Detective Ponderosa realized the crime at Worthington Research might have been perpetrated by an employee, Dr. Dijon pulled Kara's résumé. Ponderosa determined that the reference phone number on the paperwork matched the number for the phone booth next to the Zelles. Then she researched the records and found that someone named "Kara Carson" was one of the missing charity volunteers; she had disappeared from the elevator 100 years prior. Ponderosa further deduced that Kara might be hiding out at the Zelles, especially as it was next door to the phone booth. Cops Lucy and Juan had been instructed to head to the hotel. Like Roger and Kara, they'd gained entry via the broken window.

Lucy pointed her gun at Kara. "One thing I can't stand are you filthy vates. You should all be dead."

Kara batted the gun away, and the two women hit, kicked, and pulled each other's hair. It was like a wrestling smackdown but grittier and less regulated.

Lucy eventually pinned Kara to the floor and tried to strangle her.

Kara watched the cop's CQ score increase from 98.7 to 98.8. Kara could barely breathe as she rummaged through her pocket for one of the syringes that Olive had given her. She got her fingers on one but could not see whether it was blue (laced with knock-out solution) or black (containing the poisonous liquid). Kara knew she could not be fussy; she would die if she did nothing. She jammed a syringe into Lucy, who immediately went limp and then unconscious.

She rolled the cop off her and checked the color of the syringe: It was blue.

Kara muttered, "Lucky lady," as she got back on her feet.

She grabbed the gun and trotted off to find Roger.

Roger finished searching the third floor. He headed up the stairwell to the fourth level, where the conference room was located. He was shocked to see that it looked exactly the same as it had during the nonprofit gala back in 2025.

The fourth floor was like a top-secret document secured within a repository. It appeared to be anchored within some sort of time capsule. He also noticed the protest signs left behind by the gate-crashing animal activists. Two had been tossed haphazardly on the floor, and the third one, which read "Animals are People Too," rested on a chair. Its sharp stake pointed out in a perilous way.

Just then, Cop Juan burst out of the stairwell and waved his gun in Roger's face. "You're a dead man, motherfucker."

Roger tackled the cop. The gun went off, blasting a hole in the ceiling. It became a tug-of-war for the weapon.

After five minutes of grappling and exchanging blows, the two men ended up near the third placard. When Roger finally got control of the gun, Juan lost his balance and fell backward into the sign, which pierced the left side of his body. The stake protruded through his lower back. He bled and was in agony but not dead.

Kara came running from the stairway and gave Roger a hug. "Oh, my gosh. Are you okay?"

Roger, feeling the embrace was a little too romantic, pulled back. "I'm fine."

Kara extracted a handful of syringes from her pocket, found a blue one, and injected the solution into Juan's arm. "This will make you feel better until the ambulance arrives."

Juan immediately passed out.

"We'd better get out of here," Roger said.

They started to leave but heard a rustling.

"Wait." Kara stopped in her tracks. "What's that?"

"Could be another cop," Roger replied. "Let's go."

"No." Kara headed into the conference room and found Bailey sitting at a table in the shadows. "Bailey, we've been worried about you."

"I pushed the button hundreds of times," Bailey replied. "I banged on the elevator. I screamed. I went to every floor in the building. Twice. I tried to hack the electrical system. I even climbed into the shaft. There was no fifty-first floor."

"They told us not to be early," Kara said. "This is early."

"I don't think I can make it till the fourth."

"Yes, you can. Come on. We have to leave. The police will be here soon."

Roger ventured to the podium and found the crib notes he had used during his gala speech. The names of the nonprofit directors were listed, just as they had been on that fateful evening. It was surreal.

Roger remembered that Anna Green, the leader of the animal group, had handed over her business card. He also recalled that she had mentioned that her home was multigenerational.

He walked to the trash can and peered inside. Lo and behold, the business card was still there, right on top. He studied it for a second, stuffed it into his pocket, and left the hotel with Kara and Bailey.

❧

Roger picked up breakfast bagels at a deli the following morning and then drove the mattress store truck to the address on Anna Green's business card. He was particularly interested in a word she had used: "multigenerational."

He and the other elevator people had spent quite a bit of time that first night trying to locate friends, relatives, relatives of friends, or even friends of friends of friends. They knocked on a lot of doors and made a good deal of phone calls. They came up empty. Roger felt it would be beneficial to find someone—anyone—who could be trusted and could give them the lowdown on this bizarre world. Plus, the vates would need a place to crash after the owner of the mattress store returned.

Roger parked the truck in front of Anna Green's former house. It was expansive with a storybook feel and had only a sprinkle of plants in the front yard. He rang the bell again and again. There was no answer.

Roger noticed letters in a mailbox next to the front door and flipped through them. They were addressed to someone named Sousa. It was not Green, so Roger figured he had once again failed to find the relative of a friend.

Roger did not know he was being watched via secret cameras by someone—a shadowy figure— in the basement of that house. This figure had a setup of computers and cutting-edge technology that looked like the control room at NASA. He was obviously not a Luddite. He was a whiz at computers, programming, state-of-the-art gadgetry, and electronics. Who was he? Was he part of the government, an anti-vate vigilante, or an eccentric who simply did not abide by the laws of the land?

The shadowy figure watched Roger step off the porch and head toward his vehicle. Then this mysterious fellow pushed a button on one of his many keyboards, which gave him a close-up of the truck. He saw "Paradise Mattress" emblazoned on the side and scribbled these words on a notepad. He observed Roger drive away before going back to his computer activities.

On a monitor, the shadowy figure watched footage of the execution of elevator people.

A monotone voice said, "Ten vates killed in Thailand by vehicle."

Ten individuals stood in the street while an army tank mowed them down.

Then the video flashed to a new scene, and the same monotone voice stated, "Seven vates killed in Algeria by hanging."

Seven bodies hung from trees. The video panned over to the bystanders, who seemed pleased with the murders.

They chanted, "Elevator people, elevator people, elevator people…"

Next, the video flashed to a scene of eleven frightened people standing in front of a wall, and the voice said, "Eleven vates killed in China by firing squad."

These individuals were subsequently shot dead by soldiers.

❦

It was another gathering of the Council of the Universe. Bones stood in the presentation area next to the customary magic screen, which seemed to be floating in the air. He was taking the magistrate's questions about the Earthling Extermination Project.

"Please give us the percentage of rescues and attempted rescues," the magistrate commanded. "And Agent Bones, I'd like for you to demonstrate your calculations."

"Approximately 3 percent attempted." Bones used a pointer to highlight symbols and numbers that appeared and disappeared on the screen at lightning speed. "But only about

1.5 percent have had success. Most of the elevator people are hiding out until the fourth."

"That's disappointing. I expected better," the magistrate replied. "It seems our little experiment is justifying extermination. Not that we were going to spare them anyway."

"The human particles on Earth are monsters," Darkon interjected. "I told you they wouldn't lift a fucking finger."

"Please, Darkon. Do not talk out of turn." The magistrate then addressed Bones. "If the majority have not engaged and have failed to show any compassion, they are worthless as specimens. They will have no relevance with respect to Phase Two."

"Well, it's possible some will engage later," Bones said. "Maybe in a few days or a week."

"You are quite the optimist, Agent Bones," the magistrate said. "I trust you will keep an eye on the situation and report back to us."

"Yes, ma'am." Bones nodded.

Sheldon raised his hand, and the magistrate motioned for him to speak. "What about the cruelty quotient? Has it helped?"

"Agent Bones," the magistrate said. "Tell us, should we do away with the cruelty quotient?"

"No. It gives the particles a sense of who to trust."

"Very well, it shall remain.... Now, we have one more agenda item."

The magistrate motioned to several attendants, who wheeled out carts full of tree branches.

"As you know, we don't normally allow food at meetings, but we are making an exception today. Sheldon recommends the new and improved food tree, and I'd like the council to provide input. We know it has life-sustaining properties, but we are still in the testing phase for taste. Please take a branch and try it. We will vote on whether the flavor needs to be adjusted."

All members of the council took bites. They smiled and nodded with approval. Some even chatted, praising the especially succulent leaves and crunchy limbs.

"It's tangy, but not spicy." Sheldon grinned. "I'd call it a winner."

"Raise your hand if you like the flavor," the magistrate ordered.

All hands went high in the air.

Chapter Ten

IT'S HELTER-SKELTER IN CLOWN TOWN

Everyone, except Roger, was hanging out in the back room of the mattress store. Keiko and Angus played cards while Bailey watched. Carl and Kara studied a map, and Ellen was reading. Bernie reviewed the store's inventory.

"You must work out a lot." Bailey flirted with Angus.

"I can bench 225." He smiled.

"I think I saw Mussolini delivering pizza yesterday," Ellen announced.

"What was his cruelty quotient?" Kara asked.

"42."

"That wasn't Mussolini."

"Where's Roger?" Keiko said.

"Getting bagels." Ellen closed her book and set it on a table.

"Okay. I need complete silence." Kara picked up the phone and dialed the Worthington Research Institute. Everyone watched her quietly.

Olive answered the call.

"Hi, Olive. This is Kara. I'm still feeling dizzy. I'm not going to be able to come in today."

"You wouldn't believe what happened. Elevator people broke in last night and sabotaged the place. The insurance company's coming this morning."

"Really?" Kara tried to sound convincing.

Olive whispered into the phone, "I think Dr. Dijon knows who the vates are, but she's being very hush-hush about it. I think the cops know, too. Anyway, we're off work until Wednesday, July fourth."

"The damage will be repaired by then?"

"No. Dr. Dijon has arranged for us to work at a substitute lab: Radensky Enterprises. It's right down the street. It's already got equipment and specimens."

Kara noted the name and then got the address from Olive, which she also jotted down. She ended the call and wrote "Radensky Enterprises" on the poster board next to the other missions.

Seconds after Olive got off the phone, Dr. Dijon confronted her. The conversation was tense.

"You weren't talking to Dr. Carson, were you?" Dr. Dijon seemed peeved.

"Uh… why?" Olive was evasive.

"Because you're fired if you were."

"No. It was… my roommate."

Dr. Dijon marched away as Olive stared at her, perplexed.

⁕

Roger arrived at the mattress store with two bags of fresh bagels.

"Food's here," Keiko announced.

"I went by an activist's house to see if one of her relatives might live there," Roger said. "But the last name at the mailbox was different."

"Why'd you want to contact them, boss?" Carl asked.

"Partly cause the owner of this store will be back in a week. We'll have nowhere to stay. I'm trying to put a plan in place."

"Can't we get a block of rooms at a hotel?" Ellen bit into a bagel.

Roger dumped a handful of $10 and $20 bills on the table. "This is all that's left, and nobody but Bernie has a job. No offense, Bernie, but you're not getting paid until the owner comes back. We're in a dire situation financially speaking."

"It isn't that dire," Kara replied.

"What do you mean?" Roger asked.

Kara grabbed her knapsack from under a bed and emptied out piles of cash. "I know you told me not to be a common thief."

"Oh, my word." Ellen was flabbergasted, as was everyone else.

"Fuck, we're rich," Angus said, elated.

"This all came from the safe? Kara, I'm so glad you didn't listen to me. Now we can rent a second truck." Roger gave her a hug.

"Since we have money for a hotel, maybe we should forget about the rescues and lay low until the fourth," Bailey suggested.

"What?" Kara was shocked to hear such callousness coming from Bailey. "You don't care about the victims?"

Kara said sarcastically to everyone, "She doesn't care about the victims. If she doesn't care, she doesn't care. People have a right not to care. Who am I to ask her to care?"

"It's not that I don't care. I just think it's risky."

"Keiko and I didn't want to get involved in this shit in the first place," Angus added.

"We can't just leave those innocent babies to be chopped into bits or shoved into an incinerator," Ellen said. "Maybe I'm a simpleton, but I'm shocked by what's going on in these places."

"They keep it secret for a reason," Carl noted. "They don't want heroes like us to get involved."

"Heroes," Kara replied. "That's the perfect word. Sorry for being testy, Bailey. I understand your point, but Roger, Ellen, and I can't do this alone. We need at least six people, or it won't work."

"You know you can count me in," Carl said. "I may be over seventy, but I've got more zip and zest than a bobsled."

"I've gone over every detail. We won't get caught." Roger bit into a bagel.

"I'm a 'yes,'" Bernie joined the conversation. "There are some things you can't un-see."

"The three of you need to make a decision. At least one of you needs to help, or we'll have to scrap the rest of the missions." Kara stared at Angus, Keiko, and Bailey. "Raise your hand if you want the victims to die and you don't want to be a hero."

"No. Kara." Roger laughed. "Raise your hand if you want to play it safe until the fourth."

"And if you get snatched while hiding in some hotel room…" Kara added. "Well, I'm sorry. We may not want to get involved."

"I guess I'll stick with the mission," Bailey said dispiritedly.

"Me too." Keiko grabbed a bagel. "I'm cool with it."

"Are you fucking kidding me, Keiko?" Angus said. "Has your brain gone all defective?"

Everyone stared at Angus, and he felt pressured. "Fine," he replied after a beat. "I'll go along for now. You dickheads are so goddamn annoying. I hate every single one of you."

Outside the mattress store, a gray van parked on the street. The shadowy figure from Anna Green's house was in the driver's seat. He stepped out of his vehicle, walked to the Paradise Mattress truck, and placed a GPS navigation device under the rear bumper. Then he returned to his van, where he checked the GPS monitor to make sure it was operating properly. It was.

♨

Roger parked the mattress store truck in front of the Load and Aim Gun Shop. He, Kara, and Ellen got out and entered the business. They did not realize it, but the shadowy figure was parked nearby, watching them.

A clerk was tabulating numbers. There were no customers in the store.

"We need some ammunition." Roger placed four revolvers on the counter; these were the weapons they'd acquired from the police officers, Paradise Mattress, and the Worthington Research Institute.

Kara and Ellen admired a pearl-colored firearm in a display case.

"Maybe we should buy this white one," Kara said. "It matches my winning smile. What do you think, Roger?"

"I don't think that would work. There's a waiting period for background checks."

"Mister, you're flat-out wrong on that one," the clerk piped up. "Background checks went out with drones and facial recognition. Twenty years ago. All that Big Brother crap's illegal."

Despite the revelation about background checks, the elevator people did not purchase the white gun, but they bought a boatload of ammunition.

They left the store and headed for their vehicle, parked just beyond two elderly women with CQs over 90 who were sitting on a bus bench. Instead of risking social interaction with the matrons—or, God forbid, triggering a dustup—the vates went out of their way to cross the street in a wide loop. They regularly made detours of this sort. Encountering those with high CQ scores was perceived as perilous.

Carl had once said, "No reason to play Russian roulette with a cyanide sandwich when you can move to a different table for a bowl of homemade soup."

As the vates crossed back over the roadway, they were almost flattened by a human-drawn carriage. Startled, they leaped onto the sidewalk in the nick of time.

The stagecoach was transporting passengers dressed in nineteenth-century finery. A conductor sat on a perch, whipping two blond, muscle-bound boys who wore frayed loincloths and grimy Oxfords. The shoes went clippety-clop on the pavement. These poor drudges ran while chained to the front of the wheeled contraption, forced to haul the load. They appeared spent. They grunted and bleated, and their backs were marred by bloody whip marks.

Kara, Roger, and Ellen froze, mortified. They remained fixated on the carriage as it clattered out of sight.

Kara reflected on how she was perpetually on edge in this deviant land—*always jumping onto the nearest sidewalk*. She felt like she was watching an invisible hand cranking the lever of a jack-in-the-box. She was constantly in anticipation mode, preparing for the pop of the lid, the emergence of the freaky jester in a floppy cloth hat.

In this world, the surprises were, without fail, tragic; they were partnered with violence, torture, and murder. They involved heart-wrenching circumstances in which Kara was powerless to help.

Kara had to stand by like a coward because outwardly interceding would be foolish. It would be hazardous to her health. Plus, jumping into the fray wouldn't help the victims anyway. Sneakiness was the only way to navigate this warped world. It was the only rational strategy for saving at least a few of the downtrodden.

Kara shook herself away from her thoughts and noticed a boutique called Jackets, Rugs & More. There were seventeenth-century buff coats and medieval leather vests in the storefront window.

"Let's check out the period clothing," she said while trotting toward the store.

She figured trying on fabulous outfits would distract her, at least temporarily, from the sight of the scantily clad vassals in chains.

Kara entered the shop, and Roger and Ellen tagged behind. Kara was aghast. The jester had once again popped out of the box. There were scores of items made from human skin. A flesh rug, hanging on the east wall, had a human head attached to it. The head was slightly shriveled; it had jewels where the eyes should have been. The mouth was in the shape of a circle, as if the person had been caught off guard at the moment of death.

On the west side of the boutique were ten impaled human heads on sticks, complete with price tags, in a display of taxidermical madness. There were banners related to duels and combat arranged around them, indicating that the skewered noggins were supposed to symbolize the trophies awarded to victors in battle.

A collection of human heads was mounted on the south wall. Signage rated them as being in "Premium Condition" and directed customers to "Inquire about hangers, screws, and bolts."

Under them were racks of "leather" clothes—jackets, skirts, pants, and vests—made from dead people's flesh.

A clerk with a CQ of 100 stepped forward. She was a teenage girl wearing 1960s flower-power attire.

Kara looked at her for a mere three seconds… before her eyesight became blurry. Then… this girl transformed into Charles Manson, complete with a beard, maniacal eyes, and a swastika on his forehead.

"Come on in," Charles Manson said. "Can I help you find something?"

"No. No," Kara repeated. "We were just looking. Thanks."

She turned and shoved Roger and Ellen out of the store with her.

Kara went off the rails on the sidewalk, just as she had with Bailey at the mattress store.

"Mass killers for one thousand, Alex." She spoke with great emotion while imitating different characters from the *Jeopardy!* game show. "A hippie who sells human heads… . Who is Charles Manson? Ding. Ding. You are correct Kara Carson. The crowd roars."

Roger whispered to Ellen, "I think she's going mad."

"Helter-skelter can put bats in your hat. That's for sure," Ellen replied.

The next stop was a truck leasing company, where the three vates were handed the keys to a white 18-wheeler. They rented it for a week.

The final destination was a bookstore, where Kara bought *Secrets of Lockpicking*. She wanted to brush up on gaining entry into buildings, a skill she had learned from her dad during their adventures related to pretend sleuthing.

While Kara purchased the book, Roger and Ellen perused

the Recommended section. They saw the following titles: *Rebels Against the Future, Surveillance Society*, and *Why Privacy Matters*. There was also a cookbook called *Holiday Meals*. Roger and Ellen were shocked by the cover, which depicted a cooked human head and bust on a Thanksgiving platter. A carrot stuck out of the cadaver's mouth.

❧

It was half an hour before curfew. The Paradise Mattress truck and the rented 18-wheeler rolled into the darkened parking lot outside On the Spot Butcher Shop. The eight elevator people, dressed in black clothing, got out of the vehicles.

Kara picked the side gate lock with ease. "Wow, that was a breeze. I should've become a criminal ages ago."

The vates crept into the courtyard with their flashlights.

"This way." Roger pointed at the first accessory building. This was the structure he had entered previously: It was a holding facility.

He whispered to Bailey, "Give me a gun."

"Oh no. I forgot to bring them. I left them on the table at the store."

Roger noticed that she was on the verge of tears. "It's okay, Bailey. Don't worry. It's all good."

The vates entered the structure to see distressed and scruffy children and young teens stuffed into much-too-small cages. The place was dusty, and it smelled like a subway urinal.

The victims peered at their intruders with panicked expressions, and some cried out or moaned. They seemed convinced that the elevator people were their executioners, ready to haul them off to the meat grinder.

"Gosh, there are so many." Kara sighed.

"Let's get them loaded," Roger said.

Then he asked Carl to check out the second accessory

building to determine whether additional people needed to be liberated.

Carl gave a military salute, clicked his heels, and navigated toward the other edifice.

The vates removed captive after captive and placed them in the trucks. It was a difficult and time-consuming ordeal. The victims had to be marshalled along with rope tied around their bodies or carried. The ropes were crucial because a good number of these youngsters were jittery. If not kept under control, they might have injured themselves trying to escape or scampered off, gotten lost on the property, and eventually been slaughtered.

After Carl peeped through the windows of the second accessory building, he returned to Roger, who was standing in the courtyard. "It's a house with a living room and a kitchen. I didn't see any victims."

Roger was happy to hear this because the vehicles were already half full. "Great. Why don't you help at the trucks?"

Carl gleefully headed toward the parking lot.

Roger went back into the structure. He was the only vate present, as the others were transporting victims through the yard or loading them.

And… that is when the weirdness happened again. Roger's eyesight went all wonky. Things became blurry, and the children and young teens suddenly appeared to be birds—all sorts of birds. There were pigeons in one section of the room, quails in another, ducks in another, and chickens in the area next to him. There were even a couple of ostriches confined in the distance. The room looked like a home for wayward birds or a penitentiary for feathered felons. There was an abundance of beaks, wings, and plumage.

Roger glanced down to see two hens crammed into a tiny cage.

One looked distraught and said, "You chopped off my friend's head. Please don't chop off mine."

"No one's gonna chop off your head," Roger answered, but then caught himself and mumbled, "Oh, my God, I'm talking to a chicken."

He turned his attention to the hen and asked her, "How do I understand you?"

She said nothing, and in fact did not seem to comprehend his words.

"The wire's cutting into my left foot," the second hen in the cage said.

"I'll get you out," Roger replied, and then muttered, "Now I'm talking to another chicken."

He leaned against a wall and closed his eyes, trying to magically will away the "fowl" images. When he opened them, pronto… all the birds morphed back into people. Roger shook his head, hoping the illusion, mirage, or daydream was gone for good. It was always nerve-racking when this happened. He had a fear, each time, that normalcy would never return.

Roger and the other vates continued to escort victims to the trucks, but not a single one of them noticed the gray van parked nearby.

The shadowy figure was spying on them. He had fully embraced his duty, or perhaps his hobby, as a watcher, a stalker, a snoop. He had a camera and took a video of the rescue. Was this evidence going to be handed over to the government? Did obtaining footage give him a personal thrill? Or did it serve some other purpose?

When the back of the mattress store truck was full, Carl, Angus, Keiko, and Bailey got into the cab section of the vehicle, pulled out of the parking lot, and disappeared down the road. As before, they planned to take the victims to a calm suburban neighborhood.

The shadowy figure did not follow. He stayed put, eyeball-ing the white 18-wheeler and waiting. It seemed he was eager for Roger and the others to emerge.

As Kara led the last two victims through the courtyard, she was confronted by a butcher dressed in checkered pajamas and brandishing a meat cleaver. His bedroom was on the top floor of the second auxiliary building, and he had been woken by noise from the rescue. He'd peered out the window. He saw the eleva-tor people stealing what he considered to be his merchandise. To a murderer like him, living breathing victims were nothing more than commodities, money in his pocket, just another sale.

The butcher was outraged over the theft and had grabbed his meat cleaver. He'd rushed downstairs into the courtyard, where he confronted Kara.

"Hey, what do you think you're doing?" He swung the blade back and forth in a menacing way.

Kara turned and stared at the butcher and… suddenly this monster turned into an even greater monster. He looked like the killer clown, John Wayne Gacy. His face was painted. There was teal pigment around his eyes and a bright red tint around his mouth. It was a nightmarish sight. This man was no longer dressed in pajamas. Instead, he wore a red-and-white-striped one-piece jumpsuit with a ruffled collar. On his head was a cap with red, white, and blue pom-poms.

He lumbered toward Kara, who tried to push the final two victims toward the side gate.

"Hurry. Hurry. Hurry," she said to them.

The clown grabbed Kara's arm and threw her against the wall. He reared back with his meat cleaver, ready to slice her in half, but Roger came up behind and banged him over the head with a metal scale. The clown fell to the ground, unconscious.

Kara watched him transform back into a butcher. She was trembling.

"Let's go." Roger shoved Kara and the final two victims through the gate.

Bernie and Ellen were already in the cab of the truck. After the victims were loaded, Kara and Roger jumped inside the vehicle, and off they went.

The shadowy figure was still capturing video.

Kara was able to calm down as they got closer to the suburbs. "I think he was supposed to be John Wayne Gacy, the killer clown. Did any of you see that?"

Ellen and Bernie had no idea what she was talking about, but Roger replied, "I saw a clown with a knife. Who's John Wayne Gacy?"

"He was a mass murderer," Kara replied. "He died by lethal injection in the nineties."

"Did you see the birds?" Roger asked.

Everyone shook their heads.

Roger explained that the captives in the accessory building had, at one point, looked like all sorts of feathered creatures: ostriches, ducks, chickens, quails, and pigeons.

As usual, Kara felt compelled to explore the symbolism. "Birds represent the future and the past, which could be a metaphor for time travel. They also characterize the desire to become angelic, which is, of course, compatible with our rescues. The ostrich symbolizes strength through hardship."

"We've been through a lot of fucking hardship." Bernie sighed.

"Hens represent mystery and magic," Kara continued. "They were honored by Polynesian boatmen in the twelfth century."

"Magic or not, I'm flat-out spooked by this game of now you see me, now you don't," Ellen said. "I just want to get the hell out of clown town."

Chapter Eleven

WHO'S THAT NAZI IN THE WINDOW?

The shadowy figure was in his van across the street from a small industrial park. The red dot on his GPS monitor revealed that he was located near the mattress store truck, which was in his line of sight and parked next to the 18-wheeler.

He checked to make sure his AR-15 was loaded before setting it aside and using binoculars to peer at the roof of Willis Specimens, where he could make out six of the elevator people in black clothing. They moved furtively, carrying a long rope.

This man grabbed his video camera, resting on the floor in front of the passenger seat. He turned it on and propped it up on the dashboard so it could record the roof activities. Then he grabbed a hand-held computer-like device that allowed him to send text messages. He started communicating, back and forth, with another mysterious person.

He typed into the device. "Got eyes on them now. Another heist."

A message came back. "Getting footage?"

"Yep."

"Good boy. Are you sure they're vates?"

"100 percent."

"Where from?"

"Zelles."

"Cool. Keep me posted."

"Will do."

&

Angus and Bailey were at the mattress store, honoring the adage "When the cat's away, the mouse will play." They had been excused from helping with the four missions related to the vivisection breeding centers. These operations were expected to be straightforward and low volume. In other words, the vates believed there were only a handful of captives who needed to be liberated.

In return for being let off the hook, they promised to assist with the more difficult operation at Happy Farms. This undertaking was deemed more challenging because of the sheer number of victims needing aid.

Although Roger had not laid eyes inside the second ancillary building, he was pretty sure it was identical to the first. He assumed it was crammed with hundreds of abused and dejected people, awaiting a brutal and traumatizing slaughter.

Angus and Bailey invented the Baltimore Olympics in the mattress store showroom. It began with Soccer Maze, a game that required foot dribbling a ball in a zigzag pattern from one end of the room to the other. A contestant lost points when the ball hit anything, such as a bed or the wall. The first person to reach the finish line got a whopping 100 points.

They also played 50-Yard Mattress Dash, although they did not measure the distance, which was probably more like twenty yards. Angus and Bailey raced each other, jumping from bed to bed; the first person to reach the end was crowned the victor.

The final game was Mattress Mania, a takeoff on WrestleMania. This was a glorified pillow fight. The first person to fall or jump off the bed was the loser.

Angus was a pro at Mattress Mania, but Bailey routinely beat him at the other two competitions. Acting like rambunctious children was not only a way to kill time but also a distraction from their unsettling predicament.

The games deepened their friendship.

At one point, Angus collapsed on a bed, exhausted, and stared at Bailey. "You know… you're my only true friend."

"What?" She punched him softly on the arm and giggled. "I'm not gonna buy that crap. You're a stud. I know you've got tons of friends."

Angus appeared uncomfortable. "Yeah… Of course I do… I was just kidding."

While Angus and Bailey were utilizing the mattress store as an obstacle course, the other six vates—Roger, Kara, Carl, Ellen, Bernie, and Keiko—stood on the flat roof of Willis Specimens, carefully cutting the glass of a skylight. The idea was to lower Roger into the business so he could unlock the back door. Then the other five vates would dash inside and load the victims onto the two trucks.

The only unexpected deviation from the plan came when Roger was dropped into the facility and noticed a framed photo of nine scientists in white coats. Like before… his eyes became blurry, and… the scientists suddenly looked like an assemblage of Darth Vaders. They wore black clothing, black capes, and black helmets.

Roger rubbed his eyes and took a deep breath.

Seconds later, they turned back into themselves. Roger figured he should be getting used to these delusions, which were increasing in frequency, but he wasn't. They rattled him every single time.

The vates had done their homework. They visited the library and the Baltimore Department of Housing and Community Development. They perused floor plans and researched information about adjacent businesses. They bought the necessary tools for breaking and entering. They had maps, time charts, checklists, and supplies. The details were carefully crafted, and the undercover operations were designed to occur on consecutive days.

After a successful rescue from Willis Specimens, the six vates broke into a vacant hair salon. It had a "For Lease" sign on the storefront, and it was located next to their destination: Premiere Research Aids.

Roger used a high-power electric saw to cut an opening in the wall, connecting the two businesses. Then the vates crawled through the hole and liberated the caged victims, who appeared to be mostly demoralized teens.

As usual, the mysterious stranger was parked nearby in his gray van, filming the rescue.

On the third day, the target was Toskins-Wright. The vates did not wait until nightfall as they had with the other operations. They donned face masks, rushed into the business minutes before closing, and pointed guns at the staff members, who had CQ scores between 95 and 100. The employees were herded into cages while the victims were freed.

The mysterious stranger obtained footage of the vates loading up the trucks.

The break-in at Living Solutions, Inc. occurred the next day, once again shortly before closing. Kara pretended to be making a delivery. She handed a bouquet of daffodils to a receptionist; the gift was addressed to the facility's manager. Then Kara asked if she could use the restroom. The receptionist directed Kara down a hallway and left her to her own devices while delivering the bouquet.

Later, the receptionist became confused, wondering whether Kara was still in the washroom. She checked, could not find her, and assumed she had left the building.

In actuality, Kara was tucked away in a supply closet. When the business closed, and all the employees had gone, Kara sneaked out of her hiding spot and opened the door for the other vates. The victims were rescued, while the mysterious stranger once again secretly recorded their illegal activity.

These missions went down flawlessly. The vates worked in perfect harmony like slick operatives or piano notes in a mellifluous lullaby. It helped that these were easy rescues involving a manageable number of caged victims. It was like playing "Chopsticks" or "Twinkle, Twinkle Little Star" as opposed to hammering out a more complicated ballad, such as Mozart's *Piano Sonata No. 18 in D major*.

However, there was a sinking feeling among the vates that the Happy Farms mission could put their skills, coordination, and friendships to the test. And they would later learn that they were right to worry… and worry a lot.

※

It was the night of the undercover operation at Happy Farms. The mysterious stranger was again in his van, scrutinizing the red dot on his GPS monitor. The mattress store truck was just ahead, so he cautiously put his foot on the gas, hoping to ease near it without drawing attention.

He drove up the street and found the truck and the 18-wheeler parked on the side of the road, but the vates were nowhere in sight. This man parked behind the vehicles and placed his video camera in his lap, contemplating how to attain footage of their mischief. His loaded rifle rested on the passenger seat.

The eight vates could not be seen from the road because they were standing next to a back door of the Happy Farms slaughterhouse. Carl and Keiko were dressed in security officer uniforms, and the others wore black.

Kara handed Roger two blue syringes, containing the knock-out serum, and then picked the door lock like a pro.

Roger and Bernie crept inside the slaughterhouse while the others trotted into the woods.

After a trek past trees, bushes, and tall grass, Kara, Carl, Ellen, Keiko, Angus, and Bailey came to the first accessory building. They peered through the hole in the side of the structure and could see hordes of people in squalid conditions. Most had gashes and bruises.

A young woman near the opening noticed Kara and said, "It's so crowded. I can barely breathe."

"Don't worry," Kara replied. "We're here to help."

The woman cocked her head as if she did not understand.

Kara mumbled, "My God, there are so many."

The vates took turns peeking through the broken slats. Everyone noticed two Nazi officers defending the entry on the other side of the structure. They were the guards Kip and Pete—the same men Roger had seen.

"They're Nazis," Keiko said, horrified.

"Roger says they look like Nazis. Sometimes. They're not really Nazis." Carl tightened his belt because his rented security guard uniform was slightly large.

"Okay. You ready?" Keiko asked.

"Roger that," Carl replied.

Carl and Keiko headed around the building and confronted the two Nazis.

"Hey." Keiko tried to sound confident and ignore the Hitleresque appearance of these men. "JP wants to see you guys in the processing room."

"What?" Nazi Kip replied.

"JP wants to see you both in the processing room," Keiko repeated. "We're supposed to take over till you get back."

"But it's the middle of the night." Nazi Pete seemed confused. "Why would he be here in the middle of the night?"

"We just take orders," Keiko responded. "But if you don't mind pissing off JP, no skin off us. We'll just tell him you said no."

Keiko and Carl walked away.

"Wait," Kip yelled.

Keiko and Carl turned to see that Kip and Pete no longer resembled Nazis. They looked like themselves—uniformed security guards. They also seemed unsure what to do.

"I know it's nuts, but you know how JP is," Keiko added. "You definitely don't want to piss him off."

Pete and Kip decided they had better head up to Processing. They slogged up the hill toward the slaughterhouse, while Kara, Carl, Keiko, Angus, Bailey, and Ellen congregated at the entrance of the first building.

"We can't fit them in the trucks," Kara said. "There are too many. We're just gonna have to open the gates."

"Are there more over there?" Bailey pointed at the second accessory building.

"Probably," Kara replied. "Okay, Bailey, you go down the hill and open that gate. Angus, you open the other one. The rest of us will get everyone out. Once they leave the property, it will be hard for the killers to find them. There are lots of woods and fields around here."

"And a whole slew of country houses," Carl added.

"Hopefully, nice people will take them in or at least get them to a homeless shelter," Kara stated.

Bailey and Angus ran off toward the gates.

"Keiko and Ellen," Kara said. "You get everyone out of this building. Carl and I will take the other one."

Everyone got to work.

∾

Kip and Pete trudged toward the slaughterhouse, still confused about why JP would show up in the middle of the night.

"This makes no sense," Pete said.

"Well, I'm not gonna risk getting on JP's bad side," Kip countered. "I hear he killed a processor who didn't follow orders."

"I don't think that's true." Pete shook his head.

"Lots of people told me."

"How come he wasn't arrested?"

"He knows people in high places. Some of those shady politicians."

The two guards eventually reached the slaughterhouse. It was immersed in a suspicious blanket of darkness. Baffled, they entered. The place seemed quiet, much too quiet.

They stepped through the processing room door and yelled, "JP, are you here?"

"JP?"

"JP, you wanted to see us?"

The room was pitch black and strangely still.

Suddenly, Roger and Bernie jumped out, wielding guns.

"Lie down with your hands over your head," Roger ordered. "I said… on the ground, face down… Now!"

The frightened guards obeyed.

Bernie and Roger jammed blue syringes into them, and they passed out.

JP, the manager of Happy Farms, had been at home when an alarm sounded. His wife was lying next to him in bed.

He got up in his boxer shorts and stumbled over to a monitor on a desk, yawned, and hit several buttons on a keyboard, which shut off the alarm. Then he pressed several more buttons, giving him images from cameras at the Happy Farms property. He saw Roger and Bernie inside the processing room and the other elevator people at the first ancillary building. JP cursed as he picked up the phone and pressed a number.

"Hey, some criminals broke in. Get the boys and meet me there."

He ended the call and spoke to his wife, who was still asleep in bed. "You nagged me over and over about those illegal cameras. Now they're paying off big-time."

His wife turned over and muttered, "Are you talking to me?"

She went back to sleep.

⌘

Ellen and Keiko opened the doors to the first accessory building at the Happy Farms facility. They watched euphoric men, women, and children flock out of the structure and barrel toward the open gates. Kara and Carl did the same in the second structure.

"People, let's move it." Carl nudged some of the victims out of the building. "It's balls to the wall. This is your lucky day."

Kara spoke to a teenage girl and stroked her hair. "Come on, sweetie. Time to go."

Then... suddenly Kara's vision became blurry and the girl

looked like a beautiful white horse. Kara found herself stroking the animal's mane.

"We don't have to stay?" the horse asked.

"That's right," Kara replied. "You're leaving right now."

The animal did not seem to understand, so Kara led her to the exit and motioned for her to run.

"Thank you. Thank you so much." The filly trotted out the door and down the hill.

Kara watched all the running people morph into galloping horses. She leaned against the wall of the structure and rubbed her eyes, confused, but the victims did not transform back into people.

Something similar had happened to Ellen and Keiko. They had been watching the last few people dart from the first accessory building when, out of the blue, these people turned into trotting horses.

Ellen furrowed her brow and asked Keiko, "Are those humans or horses?"

He shrugged.

Angus and Bailey had the same experience at the gates to the property. The victims had looked like people joyfully hightailing it to freedom, when voilà… they magically metamorphized into a stampede of equines: fillies, mares, studs, geldings, nags, colts, foals—you name it. Some were Pintos. Others were Mustangs or Thoroughbreds. Still others were Appaloosas. Their colors were assorted: black, brown, white, or even spotted.

Bailey overheard two elated mares communicating about how happy they were to be free. She was stupefied and shouted, "You're speaking English. Wait! Come back!"

The horses ignored her and dashed into the woods.

Back in the lobby area of the slaughterhouse, Roger and Bernie stood next to the peaceful farm painting and gazed out the window, hoping to see their friends. But they could only make out parts of the grassy lawn and some trees.

"It's too dark," Bernie said. "I can't see anything."

"Me neither," Roger replied.

⁓

Kara and Carl watched the final horses gallop to freedom… but when they turned… they found themselves face-to-face with processors Buck and Floyd pointing guns at them.

"Well, looky here." Buck sported hillbilly-style overalls and a plaid shirt. "We bagged ourselves some bona fide elevator people."

"We'd shoot you now, but JP… Well, shit. He's a genuine sadist," Floyd said. "He's into a slow, painful death."

"Can't blame him," Buck added. "A man's gotta have his entertainment."

He and Floyd cracked up.

"I guess you'd better call the police," Kara stated.

"Nobody's calling the police, little darling." Floyd winked at her seductively.

The processors forced the vates to walk around the building to a truck. Buck opened the rear swing doors of the vehicle to reveal that Keiko, Angus, Ellen, and Bailey had already been captured. They were shaken and sitting on the dirty floor. The semi-trailer box was empty, except for the vates, and the only illumination came from a string of tiny cargo lights.

Floyd shoved Carl. "Get in there."

"Hey, easy brother." Carl climbed into the vehicle.

"I'm not your brother." Floyd pushed Kara toward the truck. "You, too, pumpkin."

Once Kara and Carl were inside, Floyd closed the rear doors.

"I see they got you, too," Ellen said.

"Now what do you suggest, Einstein?" Angus stared at Kara.

Bailey wiped her tears.

Kara pulled the needles from her pocket and doled them out. "I have these syringes. There are six black ones. One for each of us. They kill instantly. You can use them as a weapon or, well, you know, if things get too tough."

"You want us to commit suicide?" Angus shouted. "Are you crazy?"

"I'm just giving you options," Kara replied.

"Keiko, Bailey, and I wanted to mind our own fucking business, but no," Angus added. "All of you wanted us to risk our lives for a bunch of deadbeat strangers, or maybe they're horses. I don't have a goddamn clue."

"I wonder where Roger and Bernie are," Kara said.

With that, the rear swing doors of the truck flew open. Jed, Buck, and Floyd shoved Roger and Bernie inside. But there was one huge difference: Now the processors resembled Nazis, complete with swastika armbands and Third Reich visor caps.

Jed slammed the rear doors of the truck, and the vates endured a bumpy ride up the road toward the slaughterhouse.

"We're gonna be killed by flipping Nazis." Ellen sighed.

The truck eventually stopped, and Nazi Tanner opened the back swing doors. Jed, Buck, and Floyd, still dressed in their Third Reich attire, had guns.

JP was present; he resembled the head honcho himself: Adolf Hitler. He had a short black mustache, and his plastered black hair swept over his forehead from right to left like the slant of a German salute.

"Gee whiz." Nazi Tanner laughed. "Who would have thunk it? It's Mr. Bad Shoulder."

"You understand we can't let you go," the Fuhrer said. "Terrorists are terrorists. Get them out of the truck, boys."

The Hitleresque heavies were rough with the vates, shoving them through the back door of the slaughterhouse and into a room that contained sinks, gloves, aprons, boots, plastic containers, an assortment of knives, and a sign that read "Wash your hands after skinning."

Nazi Floyd pointed the gun at Kara. "Come with me, babycakes."

He shoved her toward a bathroom.

"No," Kara yelled. "Get off me."

"Come on, Floyd," Nazi Buck said. "Vates are dirty aliens. Why would you want to mess with that?"

"Yeah, we're dirty aliens," Roger added. "You should leave her alone."

Floyd would not let up, so Roger tried to tackle him, but the Nazis restrained Roger.

Floyd wrestled Kara into the bathroom and slammed the door.

Angus figured death was inevitable, so he sneaked the black syringe out of his jacket pocket and placed it against his skin. There were tears in his eyes. He tried with all his might but could not bring himself to use it, so he stashed it back in his pocket.

In the bathroom, Nazi Floyd ripped Kara's shirt and tried to kiss her. They struggled, and she slapped him.

"You're just like my little sister." Floyd laughed.

He threw Kara to the ground, got on top of her, and once again tried to give her a smooch.

Kara felt around in her pocket and pulled out a syringe, unsure whether it was knockout blue or the death-inducing black. She jammed it into Floyd's neck, injecting him with the serum. He fell over onto his back.

She stood and checked the color. "It's black. The color of your heart, you scumbag."

Kara carefully peered out the door and saw no one. She tiptoed through the skinning room, but Buck and Jed grabbed her from behind.

Jed, confused about Floyd's absence, ran to the bathroom and found his slain friend on the floor.

He screamed, "Shit. He's fucking dead. The bitch killed him."

Kara was dragged into an adjacent skinning area, where she found her friends standing next to a conveyor belt. Shackles were secured around their wrists and ankles; these shackles were attached via cables to contraptions near the ceiling.

"The cunt's gonna die first cause she killed Floyd," Tanner said.

All of the Nazis, including the Fuhrer, were present.

Buck clamped shackles around Kara's wrists and ankles. Then he pushed a lever, and she was flipped upside down and lifted onto the conveyor belt—a maneuver that caused her great pain. She ended up lying on her back with her arms and legs in the air like an upside-down insect.

A strap jetted across her stomach, holding her in place. Nazi Jed placed a bolt gun up to Kara's temple, ready to blast her into the stratosphere.

Hitler stopped him.

"No. I want them fully conscious when their heads come off."

Jed put down the bolt gun.

"I didn't even want to do this." Angus sobbed. "They forced me."

"You're gonna get in big trouble." Keiko struggled to get out of the shackles.

"Yeah," Angus added. "Our father will track you down."

"Please let us go," Bailey pleaded. "We won't tell anyone."

Ellen screamed uncontrollably, "Help! Help! Somebody. Help!"

Tanner placed the bolt gun against her temple and growled, "Shut up, lady."

She obeyed.

Minutes later, all the elevator people had been flipped onto their backs and securely fastened to the conveyor belt via the stomach strap. A lever was pushed, and they moved from the skinning area into Processing.

The Nazis grinned as the elevator people were transported into the room, one after the other. It was as if the helpless vates were their carefully crafted masterpiece, something they were proud of.

Kara was the first in line. Tanner pushed a button, and the conveyor belt stopped. She was within six feet of the beheading station.

"Hey, assholes," Nazi Buck said to his buddies. "Let's start the party."

He switched on a chain saw and ran it close to Kara's face.

She screeched and tried to stretch her head away.

Buck chuckled. Then he moved to Roger, who was second in line, and cut off the top of his shoe but was dismayed when he found no blood.

"No fucking toes?" Buck scowled. "Shit. Those shoes are too big for you, dickface."

Then Buck cut off a chunk of Ellen's hair and held it high. "A new rug for you, Jeddy boy."

Buck and the other Nazis laughed at the toupee joke. Then they joined in with their own versions of taunting and crude insults.

"Put it down, Buck," Hitler ordered.

Buck turned off the chain saw and placed it on the floor.

"All right, boys. It's time to launch the mother of all roller coasters."

"The carcass coaster!" Nazi Buck shouted with glee.

"You want to do the honors, JP?" Tanner asked.

"Does a king let his minions have all the fun?" Hitler grinned and pressed a button, and a motor roared.

The eight vates started moving toward death. They screamed, squirmed, begged, and cried. Some were even praying.

"Dear God," Bernie said. "Please save us…"

"This wasn't my fault," Angus pleaded.

Kara was the first in line to die, and when she moved within three feet of the beheading machine, the shadowy figure burst into the room with his AR-15 and mowed down all the Nazis. Then he pushed a button marked "Stop."

Kara was only inches from death when the conveyor belt halted. The guillotine blade slammed down, barely missing the top of her head.

The shadowy figure pushed a lever labeled "Emergency Release," which unlocked the shackles and straps.

The vates were relieved as they climbed off the conveyor belt.

"Who are you?" Kara asked, noticing this stranger had a CQ score of only two.

"Miles."

"Thanks for saving us, Miles." She smiled.

"I can't believe you have a cruelty quotient of two," Roger said. "I haven't seen anyone under twenty-five."

"I haven't seen anyone under thirty-one," Bailey added.

"What's a cruelty quotient?" Miles asked.

"It's the number on your chest," Kara replied.

Miles looked down. "I don't see anything."

"I think only we can see it," Kara said.

"You mean only elevator people can see it?" Miles asked.

The vates stared at each other, reluctant to confess the truth.

"I know you're elevator people. You disappeared from the Zelles Hotel in 2025." Miles stared at Roger. "When you showed up at my house the other day, I thought you were a government spook investigating me. Later, I realized you were a vate."

"Are you related to Anna?" Roger probed.

"She was my grandmother. We'd better get out of here." Miles pointed at the ceiling. "They have cameras. The cops are probably on their way."

"We have 84,000 questions," Kara said.

"Sorry. They'll have to wait till tomorrow. I get headaches when I don't get enough sleep. How about nine in the morning? My place."

"Okay. Okay," Kara replied. "Just two questions."

"What?" Miles sighed.

Kara pointed at the dead men. "Are they wearing Nazi uniforms?"

Miles looked at her as if she was nuts. "No. What's your second question?"

"Do they kill people here? Or horses?"

Miles once again stared at Kara like she was bonkers. "Horses."

"Ugh," Ellen said. "All those poor horses who died."

"Why would anybody kill horses?" Kara asked.

Miles climbed onto his soapbox—a posture he rather enjoyed. It always felt like one big exhale, a way to cleanse his heart, a chance to make an impact.

"They torture and mutilate them for horse meat. Horse meat is popular in Asia and Europe. Shoes and clothing are made out of their skin. Yes, it's sickening and the monsters who do this should be fucking dead. Oh wait. Good news." Miles pointed at the corpses. "They are dead."

He raised his arms in a victory stance and marched out the door.

Roger laughed. "He's just like his grandma."

Chapter Twelve

MILES AWAY FROM HOME

The mysterious stranger was Miles Sousa, a former technology expert for the U.S. government. He had a Top Secret/Sensitive Information clearance when he quit his job.

His wife had recently died while giving birth, and his infant son had not survived either. Although Miles was inconsolably upset over the loss of his family, he could have eventually returned to his job. But he had no interest. His leave of absence turned into retirement.

Miles had enough inheritance and savings to meet his daily needs, and he disapproved of how the government took advantage of the citizenry. They secretly used technology to spy, make weaponry, and control the masses while pretending they were as Luddite-minded as the average Joe. Miles had a distaste for this.

He'd stayed off the radar for months but joined the underground resistance when elevator people arrived on the scene. Miles and his buddies became obsessed with finding out who these newcomers were and why they were there.

Miles was good-looking and athletic; he could have earned his living as a professional football player in his younger days. He was now forty-one and had no relatives, except a distant cousin he had never met.

His grandmother, Anna, became the executive director of a prominent animal advocacy group at age twenty. She married a man named "Sousa" and changed her last name to match. She and her husband had a son who took a young bride late in life, and the couple had been blessed with one child: Miles.

Miles's father had been an engineer and technology whiz and had taught his son the ins and outs of the trade. As early as age ten, Miles revealed an inborn aptitude for computers, programming, and applied science. However, these skills did not lend themselves to employment, except within the government sector because the "wreck tech" movement was in full swing.

Most ordinary folks were proud to be "wrecks." But Miles was not a Luddite. He had a techie mind and yearned to use it. From an early age, he knew that if he wanted to work with cutting-edge gadgetry, there was only one way: to become an employee of the U.S. government. So, public service became his career path.

Miles was excited to host elevator people at his home. This was something his underground buddies could only dream about.

Kara, Roger, Ellen, Carl, Angus, Bailey, and Keiko rang the bell. Bernie was at the mattress store.

Miles opened the door, grabbed the mail, and led them to his den. There were nice-to-get-to-know-you handshakes and the usual amount of cordial chitchat. Then everyone except Kara and Miles congregated on the far side of the room to peruse the slew of family photos on the wall.

Miles's two miniature pigs dashed into the den, wagging their tails.

Kara squatted to pet the animals. "Oh, how cute. Are these pigs or… ?"

She stopped short and glanced up at Miles, waiting for an answer.

He stared at Kara bewildered, wondering if she was mentally unwell. He said, "They're rescue pigs. This is Sammy and Miss Pringles."

"Hi, Sammy and Miss Pringles." Kara continued to rub them. Miles smiled and crouched to give the pigs some loving strokes as well.

Suddenly, Kara heard Miss Pringles tell Miles, "We love you, Daddy."

Kara was astonished and jumped up. "Did you hear that?"

Miles looked confused. "Hear what?"

Before Kara could respond, Roger shouted from across the room, "This is your grandmother, Anna."

Miles joined the vates at the photos. "Yeah. That's the last picture I have of her. She died in prison."

"What did she do?" Roger asked.

"She got arrested at one of her protests. She was blocking the sidewalk at some fast-food joint, so the company claimed they lost money… that she intimidated customers."

"She went to prison for that?" Keiko was astounded.

"Yep. That's all it takes. If you break the law while helping the cause, you're officially a terrorist."

"My word." Ellen shook her head.

"That's insane," Bailey added.

"When did they pass that ridiculous law?" Roger inquired.

"Back in 2006," Miles said. "It's called the Animal Enterprise Terrorism Act. Plus, there are other laws. You can't photograph at factory farms. You can't criticize the meat industry. A lot of these existed before your elevator trip. Of course, enforcement's gotten ratcheted up over the past eighty years."

"Are you part of an animal rights group?" Roger asked.

"No. No such thing anymore. Way too dangerous. Of course, there are elevator people… like you."

"People like us?" Roger was confused.

"The governments of the world are really freaked out about you guys. You're the new target. Come on. Follow me."

Kara was on the couch with the pigs, communicating in baby talk. "Speak to me in English. Say 'I love you, Daddy.'"

Miles shook his head, convinced Kara was cuckoo or, to quote his late mother, "That gal's got some serious cracks in her teapot."

He yelled for his guests to follow him to the basement.

On the way downstairs, he interrogated them about what had happened at the Zelles and how they had come to travel from 2025 to 2125.

They revealed the story about the rickety elevator and their struggle to survive for the past week and a half, but said they had no idea why they had been chosen to pop into the future, who their supernatural pilot was, and what their assignment might be… if there was one at all.

⌖

Everyone, including the miniature pigs, entered Miles's basement.

When it came to security, the room resembled a bank vault. Its steel door had three deadbolts, a padlock, and a fingerprint lock. Inside were six large monitors. Two were mounted on the wall like movie screens. There were also five computers; one was the size of a small storage shed. There were thirty drones on a bookshelf, piles of papers, unidentifiable machinery and contraptions, DVDs, videotapes, keyboards, and three gigantic work desks.

On the east wall was a chalkboard; mathematical data was scribbled on it.

A tall cabinet, which held tools, wiring, and bits of electronic equipment, was on the west wall. All in all, the place resembled the nerve center of an intelligence agency.

The north side of the room was not work related. Miles called it his "chill pit," even though the area was not sunken. It had a couch, a television, a jukebox, and a vintage pinball machine. It was his favorite place to chill.

Miles dumped his mail on a table but was curious about one item, which he opened to find a DVD. He furtively slid the DVD under some papers on a desk, as if trying to hide it from his guests.

Angus and Keiko were elated to see the pinball machine; they rushed over and started gaming. The contraption let off occasional dings, buzzes, honks, and pings.

"This is quite a setup." Roger scanned the room. "I thought this sort of technology was outlawed."

"It is. At least in the private sector," Miles replied. "Society went batshit crazy back in 2101 when studies linked smartphones and 5G to cancer, genetic damage, and neurological disorders. AI and crypto were draining energy; people couldn't even use their washing machines. Plus, 5G was making planes crash, and hackers were targeting utilities.

"Hackers were shutting down utilities?" Roger asked.

"Yep," Miles replied. "And they were detonating cell phones and electric cars. Even blowing up smart homes. Lots of people were dying. It was chaos. In addition, state and corporate surveillance were getting more and more intrusive. You know—wiretapping, satellites, data mining, biometrics. The tech titans were in cahoots with the government to censor speech. What followed were protests in the streets, violence. Tech came to a screeching halt, even got rolled back. It's called the 'wreck tech movement,' and the people who hate tech are called 'wrecks.'"

"So, the government doesn't use technology?" Roger asked.

"Well, that's their claim. The truth is… Nah… No need to go into it." Miles looked around, confused. "Hey, somebody's missing."

"Oh… Bernie," Roger responded. "He has to work at Paradise until eleven. The owner comes back today."

"We won't have a place to stay," Bailey hinted.

"It's gonna be Paradise Lost," Carl joked.

"You think we could…" Kara stared at Miles and smiled.

"Yeah," Miles answered. "You can crash here for a couple of nights. You're going back on the fourth, right?"

"How did you know?" Roger asked.

"It's common knowledge. All vates have the same date but not the same time. What's your time?"

"Ten p.m.," Roger replied.

"We're going back to 2025, right?" Kara inquired.

"How would I know?" Miles answered. "You could show up on the fourth, and the elevator could blow up."

"What?" Ellen was alarmed.

"It's gonna blow up?" Bailey asked.

"I'm not saying it's gonna happen. You're probably going back to 2025. That's what always happens in the movies."

"Exactly my point," Kara interjected.

Angus and Keiko, who were absorbed in their game, let out cheers and groans as they won and lost points.

"The Mother Teresas sure are having a good time," Ellen said.

Everyone, except Roger and Miles, wandered over to watch.

Miles whispered to Roger, "Is Kara storing too many nuts in her breadbasket?"

"What do you mean?" Roger asked.

"Did she lose all her marbles in the jungle?"

"What?" Roger asked again.

"Is she a bit off? Is there something wrong with her? You know, mentally."

"No. Why? She's super smart."

"She doesn't know what a pig is?"

Roger laughed. "Oh… it's just that we keep seeing things—"

The conversation between the two men was interrupted by a roar of delight from those on the far side of the room.

"Good job." Ellen slapped Keiko on the back.

"Keiko's got the highest score of all time," Carl trumpeted.

"Don't tell them, but that's not saying much," Miles mumbled to Roger. "I'm a lousy player, and no one's ever been on that machine except me."

Keiko approached Miles. "Hey, got any food for the victorious one?"

"Everybody," Miles announced. "There are snacks in the kitchen. Help yourself. Keep in mind, I'm vegan. No meat's allowed in the house."

"Thank goodness for that," Ellen exclaimed.

"Hey, Ellen," Kara said. "Can you bring me something low-calorie?"

Everyone left the room except Roger, Kara, and Miles.

Kara settled on the couch with the pigs, and Miles once again heard her speaking in baby talk. "What about you, Sammy? Do you know English?"

Miles shook his head, still thinking she had a screw loose.

Roger borrowed the phone to call Bernie.

"Hey. It's Roger. Bring all our stuff when you leave. And don't forget to clean up the back room for your boss.... . No. We're not going to a hotel. We're staying here tonight."

When Roger ended the call, he noticed Miles was furtively watching the DVD he had received in the mail. He clearly did not want the elevator people to see it as evidenced by the sneaky angle of the display, the low volume, and how Miles tried to cover the monitor with his body.

Roger tiptoed behind him and peered over Miles's shoulder. He saw a crowd of 100 people pointing at two men and two women with their backs against a wall.

There was a male voiceover. "Four vates in Pakistan killed by bullets."

The cultish crowd shouted, "Elevator people. Elevator people. Elevator people... ."

Then the four people were shot dead.

The footage shifted to a different scenario, and the male voice announced, "Four vates in Canada killed by knives." On the screen, eight men rushed toward four people and stabbed them repeatedly with knives.

Next, the video flashed to a scene in which six people were tied to wooden stakes. The male voice said, "Six vates in Chile killed by fire." Gasoline was poured around the victims, and they went up in flames.

The following scenario involved ten people who were pushed into a chamber. The door was shut and locked. The male voice said, "Ten vates in Scotland killed by gas."

The crowd outside the chamber shouted, "Elevator people. Elevator people... ."

Miles noticed Roger was peering over his shoulder, so he stopped the video. "Sorry. I didn't mean for you to see that."

"It's hard to believe," Roger said. "Why are people so savage? Just because we're outsiders?"

"You're a threat to society, to people's way of life. It's not so different from the Inquisition. Heretics were killed for disagreeing with the authorities."

"How did you get this video?" Roger asked.

"From my underground network. We share info."

"What are they doing with the people in jail?"

"They're dissecting the dead vates. And subjecting the prisoners to all sorts of nasty tests. They're looking for the key to time travel. They're trying to find out what makes you guys different from normal people."

"Really?" Roger was horrified.

Bailey, Carl, Ellen, Angus, and Keiko returned with pretzels, oranges, carrots, celery, cookies, cake, and bottles of water.

"There's too much healthy stuff in your fridge," Keiko said.

"It took a lot of effort to hone in on the junk food," Carl joked.

Snacks were distributed among the group.

"I've got to ask you the $64,000 question," Kara told Miles.

"What's that?"

"When did people start eating people?"

"And how do you decide which people are slaves?" Keiko asked.

"Does it have anything to do with status or income?" Angus interjected.

"Do they use criminals from death row?" Bernie tore open a bag of pretzels.

"Wait. Wait. Wait. What are you talking about?" Miles asked.

"We've seen people being killed for food," Roger said.

"Where?"

"On the Spot Butcher Shop and the First Street Deli," Roger replied.

"We've been saving people's lives for the past week," Angus said. "We're fucking heroes."

"I've been following you for the past week," Miles replied. "You've been rescuing puppies, mice, kittens, rabbits, hens, pigs, monkeys. Not humans."

The vates were in disbelief.

"What?"

"No way!"

"You're kidding?"

"That can't be right," Ellen stated.

"That's a goddamn lie," Angus said.

"They look like people to us," Kara explained. "Although sometimes they do change into animals. Our eyesight's been really wonky ever since we got here."

"It's starting to make sense," Miles reasoned. "My pals in the underground kept telling me that some of the vates in jail said people were being eaten."

"This is a bunch of baloney. Those were not animals we saved, and we're fucking heroes." Angus strolled back toward the pinball machine.

"I agree," Miles replied. "You're a hero. You're all heroes. Species is irrelevant. Let me show you some footage."

The vates gathered around the computer. Miles pushed a button. Footage appeared on the screen, revealing the elevator people in a suburb releasing kittens from the back of the mattress store truck.

"Goodness gracious," Ellen exclaimed. "That's me."

"Those are cats." Carl was stunned. "Jeepers, I definitely didn't think they were cats."

Miles fast-forwarded the footage to show Kara carrying a rabbit to the 18-wheeler.

"I never saw a rabbit," Kara said. "How could I be carrying one?"

"The animals can talk, too," Bailey added.

"That's right," Roger stated. "Two chickens talked to me."

"I heard Miss Pringles speak English in your living room," Kara added.

"What does all this mean?" Roger stared at Miles.

"No idea. I just work here. I didn't bring you into the future or tamper with your eyesight. But it seems like you have a pretty cool talent. I'd love to be able to talk to Miss Pringles and find out where she hid my toothbrush. I know she's got it stashed somewhere."

Chapter Thirteen

RUN, SPOT, RUN

The 18-wheeler, parked in Miles's driveway, served as a hideaway. Kara sat alone in the cab. She didn't want her friends to see her anguish. She had to be strong.

Her father once told her that life was a dinghy on the high seas, and it was her job to be the anchor. It was in her genes. He'd said, "You're heady like me. We're not emotional bobbleheads like everyone else."

It was Kara's destiny to keep other people even-keeled and sane, to keep them grounded. But she couldn't do it this time. She felt like the anchor was pulling her under, drowning her. She had lost control of her rational side.

Her turmoil had to do with the "revelation" and a brief follow-up conversation with Miles. She'd asked, "What we saw… all that torture… the killing… behind closed doors. Was that happening to animals back in 2025?"

"Yes, ma'am," Miles replied matter-of-factly, then turned his attention back to his computer.

Kara stood there motionless. It was as if she'd been hit in the head with a shovel.

She found her way out to the truck to process her pain.

Ten minutes later, Roger exited Miles's house and opened the vehicle door. "What are you doing out here?"

Kara rotated, so he couldn't see her face.

"Hey, what's the matter?"

Kara couldn't speak because she was on the verge—the verge of spinning out of control. Roger's voice triggered more emotion than she was used to experiencing. If she looked in his direction, she knew her grief would gush out. Kara frowned and squinted, trying to hold back, determined to be contained. But then she caught a glimpse of his face, and the dam broke. She released a loud and messy avalanche of tears.

"Oh no… Kara." Roger slid into the vehicle and wrapped his arms around her. "What's the matter?"

He wiped the tears from her cheekbones with his fingers. "Tell me what's wrong."

"I wish it had been people. I wish they were the ones being killed."

"Why?"

"Because I wouldn't feel guilty. I wouldn't be a hypocrite."

"What are you talking about?"

"Everything I learned was wrong. I feel like I've been in a cult. I've been an oppressor, and I was just too stupid to see it."

"From one cult member to another, I think you're being hard on yourself. And you're not stupid, Kara. You're the only walking web browser I know."

Kara tried to pull herself together. "How do *you* feel about what Miles said?"

"About the truth? About what goes on?"

She nodded.

"Well, I knew, but I didn't know. I didn't want to know. Now I *really* know. But I've decided to be practical, to give myself a fresh start."

"A… fresh… start…" Kara repeated his words, letting the idea simmer in her head.

"We've been Luddites. Now we're upgrading our software. And when we get back home, we'll be technologically advanced. We'll be self-driving cars."

"Self-driving cars." Kara chuckled. "I like that."

Kara and Roger smiled at each other; they had finally connected.

"What's the first thing you're gonna do when you get back?" she asked.

"Get a divorce."

"What? Why?"

"My wife's been having an affair. She only married me because I was there. I was available. She treats me like one of her real estate signs. She puts me in the closet most of the time and only advertises me when she needs a plus-one for a party or when she wants to tell society that she is respectable—a wife."

"Wow, I'm so sorry. I didn't know."

"Nobody knows. I'm just tired of being signage. This time travel thing has made me realize there's a lot more to life than being boring and predictable."

"You've never been boring or predictable… I mean, you were almost a senior gopher."

They laughed and stared at each other again.

Roger broke the silence. "Well… the others are gonna

wonder where we are. Want to head back inside or spend five minutes doing the chicken?"

"The chicken?"

"Yeah." Roger turned on the radio, and the song "Put on a Happy Face" blared.

He flapped his arms to the tune of the beat.

Kara grinned and joined the silliness.

⌀

Kara and Roger entered Miles's kitchen to find the crew making cookies. Ingredients were strewn out on the countertop: flour, chocolate chips, sugar, oat milk, baking soda, vanilla extract, and margarine. There were dirty bowls in the sink and two sheets of already-baked Toll House cookies on the table.

Carl wore a frilly salmon-colored apron; he was playing Suzy Homemaker, scrubbing down the surfaces with a sponge. Sammy and Miss Pringles were curled up in their dog beds. Kara sat at the table next to Miles; she was pensive and aloof, still feeling emotional.

Keiko juggled two serving spoons in the air for a full fifteen seconds—before they came crashing to the floor. Bailey laughed and clapped.

"You want to lick the bowl, spoon man?" Carl asked.

"I could go for some cookies." Keiko grabbed a couple from a tray.

"I'll lick the bowl," Bailey said.

Carl handed it to her.

"This whole thing must be about animal cruelty. About how people harm other species." Ellen snapped the margarine lid back in place.

"Yeah," Roger said. "Seems like it's related to morality."

"What's the matter, Kara? Are you okay?" Ellen noticed that she was not her usual self.

"Yeah. I'm fine."

"So, why do *you* think we were brought here?" Ellen asked.

"My theory is… They duped us by changing our eyesight, so we'd have empathy, so we'd open our eyes and stop being prejudiced," Kara said. "They want us to look outside our species."

"I bet dollars to doodle dogs we're supposed to go back to 2025 and knock some sense into this screwed-up planet." Carl stuffed chocolate chip packaging into the trash.

"I agree. It's the only thing I can figure," Kara replied. "I'm optimistic. I think we can convince them to change."

"Good luck with that," Miles said sarcastically. "I'm sure if you just talk to people real nice."

Several of the vates laughed.

"Buddha probably brought us here," Ellen guessed. "He teaches that sentient beings should be treated with respect and compassion."

"Give me a break. There's no Buddha. There's no God or Allah either. Religion's about controlling the public." Angus crammed a cookie into his mouth.

"It's the opium of the masses," Keiko added.

"Then who do you think is behind this?" Roger directed the question at Angus.

"I don't have a fucking clue. Maybe some tech wizard invented a time machine, and we're his goddamn guinea pigs."

"He's probably listening right now and laughing at us," Keiko said.

"Anyway, it doesn't matter. I just want to go back to fucking 2025. I don't give a rat's ass about animals." Angus wolfed down another cookie.

"I want to go home, too," Bailey added. "I don't mind taking a message back, but I'm not really an animal person."

"If we're being honest, I've never been all that thrilled with human beings," Ellen admitted. "People are such assholes. I like animals better."

"People *are* animals," Miles said.

"True," Kara noted. "Jacques Derrida said that when you use the word 'animal' to separate other living beings from people, you've already started to enclose the animal in a cage."

"You're well-read." Miles smiled at Kara. "I'm impressed."

"That's why we call her Einstein. She has jumper cables linked to her brain." Roger winked at Kara.

She beamed. She liked having two cute guys fawning over her.

Then Kara turned to Miles. "It must be hard for you to live in this society. I mean, you're an animal advocate. You have an entirely different value system from everyone else. You have to look at corpses and suffering all the time. And you're helpless to do anything about it. You must feel like an outcast, an alien."

"Yep." Miles nodded. "So, what's the plan for tonight?"

"Tonight?" Roger asked.

"You've had a rescue every night this week," Miles continued. "I assume you have something planned."

The vates stared at each other for a beat; they seemed hesitant to reveal the next mission.

"Well… we're supposed to go to a lab," Kara said. "Radensky Enterprises. Ever heard of it?"

"Sure," Miles replied. "It's disgusting. Last I heard, they were burning the eyeballs out of two-month-old puppies and drilling holes in their skulls."

"What?" Kara was horrified.

"Oh, my gosh," Ellen exclaimed.

"They tend to use beagles because they're so sweet," Miles added. "You can torture them, and they'll still lick your face."

"I don't know about the rest of you," Kara said. "But I'm game for tonight."

Everyone stared at Roger, curious whether he would endorse the mission.

"We've got a solid plan," Roger said. "I think we can pull it off."

"You can count me in, governor." Carl saluted Roger.

"I've spent my life in a satin sleep mask," Ellen said. "I like seeing the sunshine."

"You're living the rebel life, Ellen." Kara smiled.

"Damn straight, I am."

"What about the three of you?" Kara stared at Angus, Keiko, and Bailey.

"You have six people, including Miles, so you don't really need us," Bailey mumbled, "I think I'll just stay here and read a book. If you don't mind."

"I don't give a fuck about animals," Angus said. "God made people superior so we can do whatever we want to anything on the planet. We can burn their eyeballs out if we want. We can fill up the ocean with goddamn garbage. We have fucking dominion. Keiko and I want our cut of the money. We're gonna get a hotel and a massage… and have steak for dinner."

"You're such a self-absorbed ass," Kara said.

"Don't you have any sympathy for those poor babies?" Ellen stared at Angus.

"Kid…" Carl said. "Roger should have left you in that meat locker."

"I don't care what any of you think," Angus said. "Keiko and I want our cut. Now give us our fucking money."

Kara went to her knapsack and divvied up the cash. She handed Angus, Keiko, and Bailey their share of the loot. Angus and Keiko left the house, just as Bernie arrived.

Bernie had lucked out; he had barely avoided arrest. Two hours earlier, he had cleaned up at the mattress store; this included stuffing the poster boards, which listed the undercover missions, into a trash can. He had lit a match and set the contents on fire.

Mr. Pebblebrook arrived shortly thereafter and paid him for a job well done. A mere five minutes after Bernie left the business for good, Detective Julie Ponderosa and several officers from the Baltimore Police Department descended on the store with a search warrant.

Ponderosa decided to investigate the mattress store based on what she learned at Happy Farms. After arriving at the slaughterhouse, she had interviewed guards, Kip and Pete, who were no longer under the spell of the knockout serum. Then she reviewed video footage of the street outside the facility and saw the truck emblazoned with the words "Paradise Mattress." She ascertained there was a link.

At the mattress store, Ponderosa rifled through the trash can. Among the burned papers, she found wording that was still legible: "The Zoo." She got on her walkie-talkie and ordered a contingent of officers to dispatch immediately to the Baltimore Zoo.

She growled into her police radio, "I'm gonna catch those slimy terrorists if it's the last damn thing I ever do."

⤳

Carl parked the 18-wheeler on the loading dock outside Radensky Enterprises. Kara, Roger, Miles, and Bernie strutted through the front door of the business wearing white lab coats and carrying medical bags. It was a minute before closing.

The vates came face-to-face with two researchers: Darla and Rosa. Both had CQ scores of 100.

"Hello," Darla said. "May I help you?"

"Hi." Kara smiled. "We're here for the inspection."

"What inspection?" Darla looked confused.

"We're with Worthington Research, and Dr. Dijon asked us

to examine the specimens in advance of July fourth. We have to make sure the animals aren't contaminated. We wouldn't want our experiments to be compromised or deemed invalid."

"I haven't heard anything about an inspection." Darla turned to Rosa. "Did Dr. Dijon say anything to you?"

Rosa shook her head.

"It's a quick process," Kara continued. "We'll be in and out in ten minutes."

Darla phoned Worthington Research. It was just after five p.m. With every ring-a-ling, the vates grew increasingly nervous, but they tried to appear calm and confident.

"Nobody's answering." Darla eventually ended the call. "Well… I guess it's okay, but it's closing time."

"Ten minutes, tops. I promise," Kara stated. "I know you want to get home."

Rosa opened the door to the laboratory, and the vates entered to find twenty-five beagle puppies.

"Dr. Potter," Roger said to Bernie. "You need to guard the door. We can't have distraction."

"Absolutely, doctor." Bernie gently shoved the two researchers back into the lobby area. "Sorry, ladies. But you'll have to wait out here with me." Bernie closed the door, giving his friends privacy. "At the last inspection, staff members were droning on and on about their kids and their dinner plans. It was very distracting."

Bernie did not know what else to say. There was an uncomfortable silence. He smiled at the women, but they did not return the smile.

He fiddled with the buttons on his lab coat. He looked down at the floor tile. Then he looked up at the indentations in the beige acoustic ceiling.

Finally, he blurted out, "So… could I interest either of you in a new mattress?"

"What?" Darla replied, confused.

"Oh, nothing." Bernie grinned.

There was more awkward silence.

⤜

Inside the lab, Miles examined colored wires in a box mounted on the wall. The box was labeled "Alarm" and linked up with the back exit.

"These look like dogs to me," Kara said. "What about you guys?"

Roger and Miles said in unison, "Yep."

Miles extracted side cutters from his pocket. He hesitated for a few seconds. "I'm pretty sure it's this one. Cross your fingers." He snipped a black cable while bracing for noise, but thankfully nothing happened.

Kara and Roger opened the cages and encouraged the beagles to come out.

"What's happening?" a puppy asked.

"We're liberating you, sweetheart," Kara replied, but the dog did not seem to understand.

Miles opened the back exit, which was located down a short hallway.

"Come along, little ones," Kara said as she, Roger, and Miles hustled the dogs out the door and into the truck.

Carl and Ellen stood by to help load.

Miles climbed into the rear of the vehicle and put his arms around a bunch of puppies, who showered him with kisses. His CQ went from 2 down to 1.9.

"Hey, Miles," Ellen said. "Your cruelty quotient just went down to 1.9. You're almost a perfect person."

Back in the lobby, Bernie was still sweating through an uncomfortable silence, trying not to lock eyes with Darla and

Rosa. He whistled an unrecognizable tune while shifting his body weight from one leg to the other.

Finally, there was a weak knock on the lab door. Bernie opened it a few inches and spoke privately with Roger. The door was once again shut.

"What's going on in there?" Darla sounded cross.

"They need me for a minute. I'll be right back. Don't you go anywhere."

With that, Bernie disappeared into the lab, ran to the truck, and joined the others. And off the vates went… with the now-liberated victims.

Darla and Rosa stared at each other. They stared at the closed door. Then they stared back at each other. Finally, they entered the lab to find everyone gone, including the beagle puppies.

∽

Roger drove the 18-wheeler while Miles, Kara, and Bernie sat next to him. Ellen and Carl were in the rear with the twenty-five dogs.

"Are we taking them to the Locust Point neighborhood?" Roger asked.

"No," Miles replied. "Let's go to my house."

Kara peered out the window and noticed a West Highland White Terrier wearing what looked like a red bandanna around her neck. She screamed, "Stop! Stop the truck!"

Roger put on the brakes, and she climbed out.

Kara scooped the puppy into her arms and examined the neckwear. The inscription on it read "To Kara, our warrior. From your little lambs." She could not believe it. It was her scarf. This was the little girl from Worthington Research—who was actually a fluffy white dog.

"Angel, I can't believe it's you." Kara was elated.

"I remember," the puppy said. "I remember you."

Kara climbed back into the truck with Angel, and Roger pulled away from the curb.

❧

Bones stood in the presentation section of the chamber with a wooden pointer aimed at the magic board, which, as usual, seemed to float in the air. He finished updating the Council of the Universe on the latest statistics related to the Earthling Extermination Project.

"It's a shame our experiment hasn't garnered more promising results," the magistrate said.

"I told you this would happen," Darkon yelled. "The human particles on that planet have always been selfish scumbags."

The magistrate chose to ignore the insolence and directed a question to Bones. "What about observational data?"

"That's just hearsay," Darkon interjected. "It's not relevant."

"Please, Darkon. I will have you removed from this meeting if you keep interrupting. Now, Agent Bones, how did they react when they realized the victims were not of their species? Do you have any empirical data? Any anecdotes to share?"

"Some of the earthlings reacted in a positive way. Others didn't. Some continued to rescue. Others didn't. There wasn't a pattern… if that's what you're asking."

"You don't seem to be altogether invested in your assignment," the magistrate added. "I hope I won't be disappointed in your management skills, Agent Bones."

"You won't be disappointed." He blurted it out much too quickly, sounding defensive.

Sheldon raised his hand, and the magistrate motioned for him to speak.

"We could have another meeting tomorrow. Some of the elevator people might spring into action tonight."

"No," the magistrate said. "This phase of our testing has concluded, and their eyesight has largely been restored. It's only two days until they return to the elevators… . Let's turn to another matter. Are the protection sleeves in place, Agent Bones? And how expansive are they?"

"Yes, they're ready to go and can be implemented four minutes prior to the return time. They have a diameter of 108 meters."

"Four minutes is much too short," the magistrate exclaimed.

"It can't be any longer due to the velocity of the casing and the density of the atmosphere," Bones continued. "But the elevator people were told not to be early for their appointments."

Darkon raised his hand, and the magistrate called on him.

"This is going to be one big botch. There's no way they can make it to the elevators in four minutes."

"I trust Agent Bones. He will figure out a way to make this work." The magistrate turned to Bones. "I'd like for you to meet personally with the elevator people who passed our little test. Your aides can meet with the others."

"Yes, ma'am."

"You, your aides, and the combat particles will need to convince everyone to complete the final phase. If not, 32,000 planets will likely die. And it will be your fault, Agent Bones."

"My fault?" Bones was freaked out. "I've never been a very convincing particle."

"You'll do fine."

"No, really. I couldn't even get my sister to stay away from the Merino Black Hole. She was missing for two hundred years."

"I have faith in you." The magistrate smiled. "Do you know how you will proceed?"

"I'll tell them they can return to their normal lives if they help with the last phase."

"Agent Bones! Have you read page 42 of the *Handbook*?" the magistrate barked. "Lying or deceiving the earthlings is forbidden. It's not what supervisors do."

"Yes, ma'am." Bones stared at his feet. He was usually a confident particle, but he seemed to turn into a pulpy mass of ineptitude when he was in front of the Council.

"You'll need to come up with something else. I'm sure you'll figure it out," the magistrate replied.

Darkon raised his hand again; the magistrate indicated that he could speak.

"Why don't we just move the barriers ourselves… instead of relying on the specimens?"

"We don't have that ability, Darkon. We only have the power to make changes to certain attributes of organic particles. We can't move inanimate objects. We're not omnipotent."

"I thought we knocked down walls on Planet Anaconda three hundred years ago," he replied.

"We did no such thing. We're just mere particles. Now go forth, Agent Bones. And bring us some good news."

Bones nodded unconvincingly and slinked out of the room. He knew he would fail; he reckoned he'd have blood on his hands. It would be all his fault when 32,000 planets ceased to exist.

He felt sick to his stomach and threw up on a nearby quasar.

Chapter Fourteen

THE TECHS VS.
THE WRECKS

It looked like a Mardi Gras celebration or a rambunctious teen pool party. There was a jubilant flurry of chaotic activity in Miles's backyard.

The Westie and beagles ran here, there and everywhere, chasing tennis balls, tussling with their friends, chewing on rubber toys, and digging in the dirt. Some even jumped into the pool, paddled to the steps, got out, and shook water droplets from their bodies. They were enjoying freedom.

The pigs, Sammy and Miss Pringles, seemed to think they were canines as they joined the fun.

Roger, Kara, Miles, Carl, and Bernie were also part of the merriment, dashing around the yard, playing with the animals, and pitching balls for them to fetch.

Ellen sat cross-legged inside a gazebo stroking

three of the puppies who had been traumatized at the research lab.

Kara had completed medical exams on these poor creatures and deemed them physically fit but had found them to be in mental distress. It would take time for them to realize their lives were no longer in jeopardy and to understand that they were loved.

Bailey was in a chair near Ellen; she ate chunks of cantaloupe and flipped through a magazine. Bowls of water and food were scattered near her feet; occasionally a dog or pig would drink or grab a mouthful of chow.

Roger called a meeting to discuss the next course of action. Miles and the vates gathered inside the gazebo.

"The zoo is the last place on our list," Roger announced.

"No," Miles said. "You have to be at the elevator in two days, and we've got to prep."

"What do you mean?" Kara asked.

"My sources say the cops plan to guard the elevators. They'll arrest as many vates as possible. Their theory is that you're aliens. They're convinced that your humanity has been replaced with something sinister and extraterrestrial."

"Really?" Bailey said. "That's weird."

"They should want us to leave," Ellen chimed in.

"If they were smart, they'd pick us up in a limo and roll out the red carpet," Kara added. "Their problems would be solved."

"Maybe they think things could get worse," Carl speculated.

"Yeah," Bernie said sarcastically. "Like we'll round up our little green friends and bring them back to tamper with their horse meat."

"I think a lot of this has to do with embarrassment," Miles speculated. "You've broken the law and stolen property. You've made law enforcement look like fools. They'll get commendations for arresting you."

"So, it's all about saving face and putting a feather in their cap?" Roger asked.

"Never underestimate the power of a feather," Miles replied.

"This is horrible," Bailey said. "We're gonna be stuck here forever."

The vates found it hard to believe that the police were guarding the elevators, so they drove past the Zelles Hotel in Miles's van. They noticed a group of cops standing near the entrance.

"They're setting up early," Miles said.

"What are we gonna do?" Roger appeared worried.

"Well…" Miles replied. "I could get you inside… on one condition."

"What's that?" Kara asked.

"Take me to the elevator with you."

"Wouldn't we be breaking the rules?" Roger said.

"Yeah," Miles countered. "Like you really give a shit about rules."

✦

Miles and the elevator people returned to the house where they enjoyed grilled vegetable sandwiches. Miles mentioned that he had friends with an animal nonprofit who would gladly care for the dogs and pigs if he were to join the others in the year 2025.

Everyone was hanging out in the basement when the doorbell rang. The vates froze, fearing the authorities had tracked them down.

Miles pushed several buttons on his keyboard, and images

appeared on a huge monitor mounted on the wall. It revealed that Angus and Keiko were standing on the porch.

"Damn, the Mother Teresas are back." Ellen shook her head.

Miles pushed another button and spoke into a microphone, "Sorry, Nobody's home."

"Let us in." Angus banged on the door. "Let us in. Or we'll tell the cops where you live."

Roger ventured upstairs and opened the front door. "You have a lot of nerve showing up here."

"Well, we have to get back to 2025," Angus replied. "You gonna leave us?"

"It's a thought," Roger mumbled, as the boys stepped inside.

Keiko pulled Roger aside, eager to find out whether the mission had been successful. The two men had a good conversation. Roger could tell Keiko was annoyed with his ogre of a brother. He seemed enthused about severing ties.

"I can help with the zoo mission." Keiko was animated and upbeat.

"We're skipping the zoo. Plus, Miles is going to the elevator with us."

"Isn't that against the rules?" Keiko asked.

✍

The elevator people were congregated in the basement watching Miles pace back and forth. He was focused and in deep thought. The vates stared at him attentively and reverently; it was so quiet you could hear a snail wriggle or a butterfly breathe. Finally, he stopped and stared at Angus and Keiko.

"Before I forget. The yard's a mess. You two are in charge of waste disposal." Then he went back to pacing.

"What the fuck?" Angus shouted.

"Shhh," Kara scolded. "He's thinking."

Angus rolled his eyes.

Finally, Miles walked to a shelf and examined a drone. "They want aliens? We'll give them aliens."

Miles compiled a list of the tasks necessary to ensure a triumphant return to the elevator, and everyone got to work. They began by renting nine matching cop uniforms from a costume shop. They looked nothing like Baltimore Police Department gear or actual law enforcement outfits. They were burgundy and appeared a little Mickey Mouse, but there was no other option.

Back in the basement, some of the vates constructed cop badges by placing slices of metal into a press and then using a computerized engraver to print the word "Police" on the star-shaped portion of the object. Other vates soldered, painted drones, or worked with lighting tubes.

The next step involved a significant amount of retrofit. Miles, dressed as a city worker, modified the lampposts adjacent to the Zelles Hotel with laser technology. With the click of a button, holograms of aliens would appear in the windows of the adjacent building. Miles hoped the wreck-tech cops would think they were being attacked by little green men.

Miles also installed heat-seeking light projectiles from the same lampposts. They could detect human bodies and thus shine red dots of light on those guarding the Zelles. The cops would suspect they were in the crosshairs of a sniper's rifle and abandon their posts.

In addition, the lampposts were outfitted with tranquilizer darts that could fire with precision up to 200 yards. By shooting one or two guards, the vates figured the others would panic and leave.

Some cops noticed Miles working at the lampposts and smiled at him. He gave them a friendly wave back to reinforce the notion that he was a city worker and authorized to be there.

Later in the day, Roger showed up dressed as a utility employee. He added miniature speakers to the phone booth in front of the Zelles. The sound would be activated via a modified cell phone, which Miles would have.

The cops noticed Roger but were not alarmed by his presence after he shot them a welcoming smile.

That evening in the basement, Miles and the elevator people modified drones by equipping them with balloons and strings of solar lights. They would resemble spaceships among the dark backdrop of the night. The plan was to fly them over the hotel at the appropriate time with hopes of scaring the cops and motivating them to flee. Other drones were designed to write in the sky, spelling out the message "Leave or you will die."

Angus had not been pulling his weight. Instead of contributing, he had been playing pinball. Ellen confronted him with her hands on her hips. The next thing you know, Angus was in the backyard picking up dog poop.

✍

It was Independence Day. This was the moment the vates had dreamt about for two long weeks. Although their appointment was scheduled for ten p.m., Miles and the elevator people felt they needed to put their plan into action early to increase the odds of success. They figured it could be tough getting past cops; breaching the vacant hotel, which was surely locked up tight; and making it into the elevator. They also assumed they would need to get to the top floor, where the blindness had occurred—a time-consuming process due to the stop-and-go nature of the lift.

It was 8:45 p.m. when the elevator people made it to a vantage point near the Zelles in their burgundy law enforcement uniforms. They noticed that the place was swarming with cops.

"We should go to the side door," Roger whispered to the others. "That'll be the easiest entry point."

"Everybody ready?" Miles asked.

The vates nodded.

"Okay. It's showtime." He punched a sequence of buttons on a contraption, resembling a remote control or a modified cell phone. Drones, which looked like spaceships with flashing lights, appeared above the hotel, along with skywriting that read "Leave or you will die."

Cops Larry and Stan, who had been at the First Street Deli, were among the officers in front of the hotel. They were alarmed when they cast their eyes upward.

Then Miles pushed another sequence of buttons, and a loud voice emanated from the phone booth, repeating, "Leave or you will die. Leave or you will die. Leave or you will die… ."

All the officers seemed confused and flustered. Some appeared afraid.

Miles pushed additional buttons on his contraption, and holograms of little green men materialized in the windows of the building across the street. Then red dots of light shone on some of the officers' bodies, making it seem as though they were in the crosshairs of high-powered rifles.

Cop Stan looked down to see the red laser beam on his chest and screamed. "Run. Larry. They've got weapons."

Cops Stan and Larry, as well as several other officers, abandoned their posts, jumped into their squad cars, and sped away.

Officers Juan and Lucy, who had chased Roger and Bernie at the Miller softball field, kept trying to dodge the tiny red dots. Finally, a tranquilizer dart hit Juan, and he fell to the ground. This freaked out many cops; several jumped in their vehicles and abandoned the hotel. There were only a handful of police remaining.

Cop Lucy shouted, "They're firing shots. Take cover."

She moved behind a wall.

Detective Ponderosa was frustrated at the doltish nature of her officers and yelled, "No. It's a trick. You have not been relieved of duty. Come back here, officers. It's just technology."

No one was listening.

She mumbled, "I'm dealing with fucking Luddites."

∾

Miles and the vates made their way to the side door of the Zelles, guarded by Randy, a police officer with a CQ of 55.9. They noticed the broken window where they had entered previously; it was covered with plywood.

"Special Agent Potter of the FBI asked us to assist." Roger had an air of self-assurance. "He wants us stationed inside the building."

Cop Randy took note of the unusual burgundy uniforms. "Where are you from?"

"Penn Police," Roger replied. "We've been called in from out of state."

Randy spoke into his walkie-talkie. "Nine officers here from Penn Police. They say they're supposed to be positioned in the building. Over."

Suddenly, there was chaos over the radio.

"They're firing weapons." Lucy's voice emanated from the walkie-talkie. "Shot my partner. It looks like some kind of... alien invasion."

Randy seemed concerned and turned up the volume on his radio. He heard the voices of various officers.

"Mayday. Mayday. Get away from the hotel."

"Shots fired. Take cover."

He turned to Roger. "Can you guard the door for a few minutes? Something's going on."

"Sure thing," Roger replied.

Randy bolted toward the front of the hotel with his gun drawn.

Miles and the vates slipped inside the building, which surprisingly was unlocked, and ran to the lobby. Kara repeatedly pushed the call button. She turned to see Detective Ponderosa peering through the entry glass; she was carrying a gun and sword.

When Ponderosa started to unlock the hotel doors, Miles and the vates bolted to the stairwell.

"Let's go to the fourth floor," Kara yelled.

On the fourth floor, Kara dashed past the animal rights signs and pressed the elevator call button over and over.

Roger, Bernie, and Miles put their weight on the stairwell door, hoping to block the cops from entering.

Detective Ponderosa, who was now in the stairway at the fourth floor with officers Angie and Burt, pushed on the door. The vates leaned into it with full force.

Finally, Kara yelled that the elevator doors were open. Miles and the vates scampered to the lift while firing shots at the stairwell so the police would not follow.

Detective Ponderosa and the other two officers cautiously made it to the lift just as the doors were gliding shut. They shot at the metal to no avail.

Inside the elevator, Roger pushed the button for the fiftieth floor. The lift moved upward.

"What time is it?" Kara asked.

"8:58," Roger replied.

"Maybe they'll take us back now," Keiko said.

"I doubt it," Kara responded. "They said not to be early."

The elevator began to squeal just as it had previously. Miles and the vates watched the display with anticipation.

Unbeknownst to them, the cops were moving up the steps, monitoring which floor they were on. They'd trudge up a few stories, check the elevator display, and then return to the stairway and keep climbing.

When the lift got to the thirtieth floor, it acted like it had before: It stopped, jerked, moved slightly upward, sputtered, creaked, and squealed. It did this again and again.

The vates gasped with each abrupt movement but were calmer than before because they knew this quirky activity was "normal."

Miles shrieked, "What's going on?"

"Don't worry," Kara said. "It does this."

The elevator reached the fiftieth floor and stopped. The vates looked at each other, puzzled.

"Now what?" Kara asked.

"I think we need to go to fifty-one." Roger pushed the "up" button.

"What time is it?" Kara inquired.

"9:15," Roger said.

"Shit." Angus sat on the ground. "We've gotta wait forty-five minutes."

Everyone plopped down on the floor to await their 10 p.m. appointment.

Thirty minutes passed.

Suddenly, there was a clanging. Someone seemed to be trying to pry open the elevator doors.

"Oh no," Kara said.

"This is Detective Ponderosa of the Baltimore Police. Come out with your hands up."

"Go to hell, lady," Ellen screamed.

"Leave us alone," Bailey shouted.

Detective Ponderosa's sword emerged in the crack between the elevator doors. Roger and Bernie drew their guns, while Kara hit the blade with the handle of her revolver, hoping to dislodge it.

The cops were able to pry the doors slightly open. When there was a one-inch gap, Ponderosa put the barrel of her gun through the opening and fired three shots. Miles and the vates scrunched up in a córner away from harm.

Suddenly, there was a freakish noise. It sounded like whales moaning followed by breaking bones. Kara put her eye up to the opening and looked into the hallway of the fiftieth floor. She watched Detective Ponderosa and the other two cops transform into eight-foot-tall sand-colored shrubs. Green leaves sprouted from their branches. Flowers, nuts, seeds, and fruit appeared. They looked like lush trees. The sword was resting on the floor.

Kara turned to her friends. "You're not gonna believe this."

⁂

Miles and the vates were ecstatic when the lift climbed to the fifty-first floor. It was 10 p.m.

The doors opened to reveal Bones, who appeared to float in the air. The vates took note of his odd appearance: his human-like eyes and mouth, his platypus-shaped nose, his batlike ears, his facial coloring like a raccoon, his whiskers like a sea otter, his thick lion's mane, hairy legs, and floppy feet shaped like those of a kangaroo. His hands and arms looked human, but his torso was shiny and silver.

Bones used a tiny comb to extract sticks and other debris from his hair.

The elevator people gave him a standing ovation.

"That's quite a welcome. Sorry to subject you to my grooming ritual, but I had to brave a heck of a monsoon. My name's Agent Bones, but you can call me Bones."

"Are you a secret agent?' Carl asked.

"No. Today, I'm more of an emissary, a messenger. I know who all of you are… except you." He stared at Miles. "What are you doing in my elevator?"

"This is Miles," Kara spoke. "His cruelty quotient's only 1.9."

"He's almost a perfect person," Ellen added.

"He helped us get past the police," Kara said.

"There wouldn't have been any police if you'd come on time. You were an hour and fifteen minutes early." Bones shook his comb at the vates. "You didn't follow instructions."

"Sorry," Kara said. "We were anxious to get back to 2025."

"You're not going back to 2025."

"What?" The elevator people shouted in unison.

"But that's what always happens in novels," Ellen said.

"This isn't a novel," Bones replied.

"You have to send us back," Kara pleaded.

"I'm afraid that isn't possible. We don't have that kind of technology."

"But you brought us here," Roger said. "You can take us back."

"You know how the rain comes down? It can't reverse direction. Our power's sort of like that."

"It's a bus with a radiator leak and half a tank of gas," Carl quipped.

"No." Bones shook his head. "It's more like the rain."

"But I can't leave my daughter," Bailey pleaded.

"What's her name?" Bones asked.

"Eva… Eva Iverson."

Bones waved his hands and a screen appeared next to him, floating in the air.

"She was with Mrs. Johnson," Bones said. "Right?"

"Yes. The babysitter. Mrs. Johnson."

An image of a girl carrying books appeared on the screen. She entered Harvard University.

"She had a good childhood, raised by adoptive parents," Bones said. "She never blamed you for disappearing. After all, it wasn't your fault. She went to Harvard and married at twenty-five."

Footage of a woman playing with two toddlers popped on the screen.

"She had two children and was a corporate executive for a swimwear company," Bones added.

Then there was a video of Eva speaking at a podium in front of a large crowd.

"She received awards for her charity work. She died at ninety, two years after her husband. She had a very good life… Anything else?"

Bailey tearfully shook her head, and Bones waved away the screen.

"We can't stay here," Roger said. "Everyone thinks we're terrorists."

"Don't worry. You'll be dead in a week."

"What?" Miles and the vates once again spoke in unison.

"Forget I said that. What's the matter with me?" Bones hit his head with his comb. "Bad Bones. Bad Bones. Why can't I follow the handbook?"

A book titled *Handbook* materialized. He consulted it and then waved it away.

"Okay," Bones continued. "You'll be dead in a week. But there's good news. Everybody else will die before you." He glanced at Miles. "Except you, Miles. You may die really soon."

"But I'm at 1.9."

"Valid point," Bones replied. "I'll put in a good word for you."

"I'm too young to die," Bailey mumbled.

"Agent Bones. Sir," Angus said. "Do you know who we are? Keiko and I are part of the Van Graff lineage."

"What he means is… We can get you ransom money," Keiko clarified.

"Boys, it doesn't matter if you're rich or poor. At the end of the day, it's bedtime."

"Why are you doing this to us?" Kara asked.

"It's all about the cruelty quotient. It's sky-high on your planet, and frankly, your species is 100 percent to blame."

"So, this is about morality?" Bernie asked. "About what people do to animals?"

"No," Bones replied. "It's not about how humans are psychopaths and treat other animals like garbage. I don't judge."

"I think you are judging," Roger said.

"Am I? Oh, sorry."

"Don't apologize, Bones," Miles said. "Humans are sadistic pricks to other species. That's sheer fact."

"I'll definitely put in a good word for you, Miles. Anyway, the Council of the Universe never judges. They're sort of like robots but with warts and fat beaks. Their decisions are purely pragmatic. Bottom line: You're screwing it up for everyone else. When the cruelty quotient on one planet is too high, other planets experience tornadoes, monsoons, hurricanes, blizzards, drought."

"We can bring our numbers down," Kara pleaded. "If you let us go back to 2025, we can get everyone to change."

Bones laughed. "You gonna join a protest or say 'pretty please'?"

"Well, it's worth a try," Kara added.

"Yeah," Bailey chimed in. "Please let us try."

"Sorry. *Homo sapiens* should have been eradicated centuries ago. The Council kept giving you a break. Actually, it was Sheldon. There's something wrong with Sheldon."

"How do you know the people on our planet are the problem?" Roger asked.

Bones once again waved the floating screen into existence. Numbers materialized on it at supersonic speed. They looked like gibberish and disappeared a second after they appeared. A wooden stick popped into Bones's hand, which he used as a pointer.

"You take the oblate spheroid with the third lemma and divide it by eight billion after subtracting the seventh and eighth ordinal numbers. You can clearly see where this is going. I don't think I need to finish the equation." The wooden stick and board vanished.

"Why'd you bring us here if you're just gonna kill us?" Ellen asked.

"Your purpose is twofold. First, you and the other 362,000 tourists are research subjects."

"You're doing research on us?" Angus shot daggers. "That's fucking unethical."

"I don't think you, as a human, have the right to talk about ethics," Bones replied.

"Bones has got a point," Miles interjected.

Bones smiled approvingly at Miles.

"What kind of research?" Kara asked.

"Tampering with your vision and communicative skills. You see, most people on your planet lack compassion for other species. We wanted to see if we could alter that. The results will come in handy if some other planet down the line goes rogue. Or devolves into relentless evil the way your species has."

"You're judging again," Roger interjected.

"Oops. My bad."

"Okay," Kara said. "We're specimens. What's the second reason we're here?"

"You have a special assignment, and you have seven days to complete it. The eight of you—and maybe Miles, if I get approval, are destined to be saints, saviors of the planet. Isn't that exciting?"

"No. I want to go home," Angus said. "I don't want to be a fucking saint."

"Mother Teresa doesn't want to be a saint," Kara quipped.

Everyone, except Angus, chuckled.

"What does saving the planet mean?" Roger asked.

"There was an eighteenth-century philosopher, Immanuel Kant. A bit of an idiot," Bones said. "You may have studied him in school. He argued that only humans were ends in themselves. Other species were tools or means to that end. We're putting Kant's theory in reverse."

"So, this is about revenge or… reparations?" Kara inquired.

"No, nothing that esoteric. We simply need worker bees to rescue those who are trapped, and you folks won the lottery."

"Lucky us," Ellen muttered.

"What do you mean by 'trapped'?" Kara asked.

"Trapped. Verb. Enslaved. Confined. Imprisoned," Bones said.

"Excuse me, Mr. Bones," Carl spoke. "Can you give us the lowdown on logistics?"

"There's a map in the pocket of your elevator."

Carl removed a map from a plastic display case attached to the wall.

"That's your district. Each group of tourists has its own district. You will release victims from homes, cages, sheds, and tanks. Leave doors and windows open. Your job is to make sure they don't starve to death. We don't want that pesky cruelty quotient to spike, now do we?"

"I don't care about your stupid cruelty quotient, and I'm not gonna help." Angus folded his arms on his chest.

"Suit yourself," Bones replied.

"I'll save the planet if you let me live," Bernie said.

"Sorry. No can do. We don't negotiate with terrorists."

Bones waited for a beat and then cracked up. "I'm just kidding. You're not terrorists."

Kara raised her hand, and Bones pointed at her as if she was a student.

"Young lady in the front row."

"Why did the police detective turn into a shrub?"

"Oh, I almost forgot. Food trees provide nourishment for the victims."

"Food trees?" Ellen asked.

"When people die, they turn into food trees. These shrubs, as you call them, are brilliantly designed because they provide nourishment for every single organism on your planet. You'll eventually be food trees, too. Isn't that cool?"

"Can't wait," Ellen said sarcastically.

"I've already added it to my bucket list," Roger stated.

"Well, Bones," Miles said. "I think it's both efficient and ingenious."

"Stop sucking up." Kara scolded Miles.

"Anyway, got to run," Bones said.

"Wait. We've got tons of other questions," Kara shouted.

"Sorry. No time. Other tourists are waiting. I won't be able to get back to you with an answer, Miles. You'll either croak in the next three or four days or die next Wednesday at noon with the others. Depends on the Council. Try not to think about it. Enjoy the rest of your vacation."

Bones vanished, and the elevator doors slammed shut.

Chapter Fifteen

PASCAL'S WAGER

Bones had informed the elevator people that they were destined to die, and he had left them to cope with their anguish and unanswered questions.

Everyone, except Carl and Miles, looked like scarecrows, wearing frozen expressions of shock and disappointment. They lacked their typical verve and chattiness. They stood quietly as the elevator descended, floor after floor. Although the contraption went through its usual squeals, sputtering, and topsy-turvy zigs and zags, everyone appeared numb.

Kara didn't care if it crashed. She felt like she was balancing on a tightrope that was about to snap, like she was trapped in a car and seconds away from exploding. She assumed her tattered emotional state mirrored that of a terminal patient who had been given unfavorable news by a physician.

Bernie eventually broke the silence, banging violently on the wall of the lift while hurling every obscenity listed in the *Oxford Dictionary of Modern Slang*. "It's not fucking fair," he screeched.

"Anger's the second stage of grief," Kara said. "It follows denial. I'm in the fourth phase: depression."

"Maybe Bones was lying," Roger conjectured. "Maybe we're not really gonna die."

"No. It would be the other way around," Kara responded. "He'd tell us we were gonna live just to get us to do his handiwork. He was being truthful… unfortunately."

The elevator continued to move down; everyone grew quiet again.

In one corner, Roger spoke to Miles, "Well… looks like I'll never see Joan again."

"Sorry, man," Miles said. "My wife died during childbirth a year ago. The baby didn't make it either. It was a tough time."

"Wow, that's devastating," Roger replied.

In a different corner, Bailey whispered to Kara, "Do you have any kids?"

"No. I've always wanted a daughter, but I have a tendency to scare men off."

"You'd be a great mom. You're so altruistic."

"There's no such thing as pure altruism." Kara leaned into her philosophical studies. "Humans are self-interested beings due to a mechanism called psychological egoism. It's just that some people feel good when they help others."

"I'm not like that," Bailey replied. "I'm not a nice person."

"Don't say that. Of course, you're a nice person."

"I didn't want to go on any of the missions. But I thought if I stayed behind, you'd think I was wicked or call me a 'Mother Teresa.'"

"I wouldn't have done that."

Bernie had calmed down from his tantrum. He was in a third corner with Carl, who seemed chipper considering the circumstances.

Carl held out his leg as if it was a trophy. "I've got a metal rod in my right thigh just north of my patella. They used to call me 'Iron Man.'"

"I thought Robert Downey Jr. was Iron Man," Bernie said.

"He stole it from me," Carl replied.

Bernie shook his head, figuring Carl was once again "being Carl."

As the elevator continued to descend, Bailey sobbed while holding her face in her hands. In a surprising act of kindness, Angus put his arms around her. It seemed as though he really cared.

"It's okay. It'll be okay," he whispered.

This was a side of Angus that no one had seen, including his brother.

The elevator finally reached the lobby, and the doors opened to reveal Officer Lucy brandishing a gun.

"Now I've got you cornered, you filthy aliens," she growled. "Turn around and put your hands on the wall."

"Really?" Kara sighed, fed up with the game of cops and robbers.

"Not again." Bernie rolled his eyes.

"Whatever." Ellen sounded like a rankled valley girl.

Miles and the elevator people were ho-hum about the command but obeyed nevertheless. Suddenly behind them they heard the moan of a whale, followed by the sound of breaking bones. They turned to witness Lucy transforming into a food tree with verdant branches and dozens of red apples.

Ellen grabbed a piece of fruit and took a bite.

"Are you sure that's safe?" Kara asked.

"Who cares?" Ellen shrugged.

Miles and the elevator people continued to chat as they traversed the lobby.

"My parents are communists," Roger said to Miles. "It's always embarrassed me. They moved to Kansas."

"Communists in Kansas?" Miles asked.

"Yep," Roger replied.

Bailey, Angus, Ellen, and Carl were clustered together, babbling about superficial topics. It was a way to take their mind off the inevitable.

"I'd be a palm tree so I could live in a warm climate," Bailey stated.

"I'd be a weeping willow," Ellen said. "It has long hair like I used to have… before the chainsaw incident."

It was Carl's turn. "I had two white birches in my front yard. They're so wispy. I just love wispiness. Let me get that for you, beautiful lady."

He held the door open for Ellen, who blushed. Then Carl smiled at Bailey and held the door for her. "And another beautiful lady."

Everyone exited the building to find something unexpected. Plants had been growing like gangbusters. Vines were climbing up buildings, beginning to encase motor vehicles, and wrapping themselves around lampposts. It was as if the eradication of humans was giving nature a reason to perk up—to spread its wings and frolic.

"Wow," Kara said. "It looks like Mother Nature has been chugging some serious caffeine."

"There are plants everywhere." Roger was stunned.

Keiko pointed at a cluster of trees sprouting out of the concrete. "I bet those were cops."

Bernie went bananas again. He rushed up to a food tree, ripped off a branch, and screamed, "I don't want to die. I don't deserve this." He looked at the heavens and pleaded, "God, how could you do this to me? Please let me go home."

Then he threw the torn limb onto the ground. It immediately turned into a full-grown food tree, shocking everyone.

"Oh, my gosh," Ellen exclaimed.

"You've got a green thumb, my boy." Carl chuckled.

The group headed home.

When they reached Miles's house, they noticed the formerly barren front yard was filled with green ivy. Plus, the foliage had climbed approximately 25 percent up the brick dwelling.

Although everyone was exhausted and wanted to get some shut-eye, they couldn't due to anxiety about their upcoming demise.

Miles passed out a fistful of sleeping pills. Everyone swallowed a couple, including Ellen, who had always been a wholesome sort; she was usually a skeptic about medication.

Miles cuddled with the pigs in his bed while the vates grabbed pillows and blankets and slept on the living room floor with the beagles.

Kara curled up in the corner with her arms around Angel, the Westie.

Worries about death were not on the menu—at least until morning. The house was filled with snoozing beings.

∽

It was morning. Miles checked the TV and radio, flipping from station to station. There was no mention of people turning into food trees. However, there were reports that police officers had staked out elevators and made arrests. Miles's underground pals were more informed than the mainstream media. They acknowledged that some humans had transformed into vegetation, although they did not understand the motive or mechanism behind the conversion. They were firm in saying that it *was* indeed happening and calling it an "alarming and freaky" development.

Miles and the vates decided to visit a pocket park in the town square to appraise the situation. They wanted to see whether citizens were in a panic or whether society was puttering along in a typical way. They also figured they could pick up some breakfast at a nearby eatery.

The group arrived to find what appeared to be six food trees in the park; one had a bird feeder. There was greenery everywhere; it was much lusher than the last time they had visited.

The public's behavior was mixed. Some people strolled in a routine fashion. Others ran to and fro in a panic. A shoe store in the distance had fallen victim to looting.

Miles asked everyone what they wanted to eat and then headed into a café.

All seemed normal inside the eatery. There was a short line.

Miles stood behind a middle-aged woman named Trish. He thought he should do his part by advocating for confined animals in accordance with Bones's request.

"Do you have any companion animals?" He struck up a conversation with Trish.

She turned and smiled. "Why, yes. I have two teacup poodles."

"You need to make sure they don't get trapped in your house because in the next few days—"

Trish noticed it was her turn to order and interrupted Miles. "Excuse me. I'm next. But I just love animals." Then she said to the clerk, "I'd like bacon and sausage with two eggs over easy."

Miles stared at her, disappointed. He knew it would be tricky to fulfill Bones's directive—that is, if the vates even wanted to help. He was unsure whether they'd choose to spend the final week of their lives in a different way, such as by meditating or having fun.

Miles carried the food back to the others, who sat at a picnic table. Everyone was present, except Kara and Angus.

"Black coffee for Bernie." Miles handed out the drinks and edibles. "Bagels and orange juice for Roger, Ellen, Bailey, and Keiko. French fries and chocolate cake for Carl."

"You're eating like it's the end of the world or something," Roger said to Carl.

Everyone chuckled.

"It's good to have a sense of humor in times of tragedy," Ellen stated.

"Where's Kara and Angus?" Miles placed the rest of the food on the table.

"Kara ran after that talking cat," Roger replied. "I have no idea where Angus is."

"He wandered off in a daze," Keiko said. "I think he's losing his grip on reality."

Ellen looked at Miles. "You must be all nerves not knowing whether you're gonna die in a week or in the next five minutes."

"Either way, no big deal." Miles took a bite of his bagel. "Actually, it's probably good if I die."

"Why would you say that?" Roger asked.

"I'm just being rational. I calculate the happiness in a world without people. No more oil spills, bombs, deforestation, global warming, nuclear accidents, billions of pounds of plastic crap in the ocean."

❧

Kara was determined to track down the black cat from Worthington Research, who had blotches of purple paint on her fur. Kara hurried down street after street, searching.

"Here, kitty," she called out. "Kitty. Kitty?'

Kara rounded a corner, and... to her surprise... found

herself face-to-face with Olive and Dr. Dijon. They stood on the sidewalk in front of Worthington Research.

"Oh… hi," Kara said uncomfortably. "Uh… how are you?"

She noticed the black-and-purple cat disappear behind a bush in the distance.

"Why are you doing this to us?" Dr. Dijon was incensed.

"Doing what?" Kara asked.

"Killing everyone. You're turning people into trees." Dr. Dijon spoke to Olive, "This is all her fault. She's an elevator person."

Olive was aghast. "You're kidding?"

"I'm not killing you. By the way, I saw your internal numbers. For vaccines, drugs, household products. Those tests you do. They're worthless. They don't extrapolate to humans. It's bad enough that you mutilate animals, but you do it for no fucking reason at all."

"So what?" Dr. Dijon became condescending. "Everybody in the industry knows results hardly ever extrapolate. We have the right to get grants, Dr. Carson. It's a human right to earn a living wage. You want us to be poor?"

"Yeah," Olive chimed in. "You want us to be poor?"

"You act so high and mighty, but you and your terrorist friends are the reason everyone's dying," Dr. Dijon said. "This is all your fault."

"No," Kara replied. "It's all *your* fault. Your cruelty quotient is through the roof, lady. But you're right about one thing. It's my fault, too. All of us fell for the nonsense fed to us by our parents, our teachers… society. We should have fought the system. We all participated in a culture of cruelty and oppression."

"I don't know what you're talking about, Dr. Carson," Dr. Dijon said. "But I know you have special powers. You're killing people, but you can spare them as well. Please save me. I'm begging you. Please."

She got on her knees while dropping a folder labeled "Research Grant" onto the pavement.

Olive imitated her boss, also falling to her knees. "Me too. Save me, too."

Passersby stared at the three women, and Kara felt embarrassed.

"Get up. Both of you. I don't have special powers. I'm gonna die just like you. I promise. I'm telling the truth."

Suddenly, Olive and Dr. Dijon lifted their chins and moaned like whales. There was the sound of breaking bones, and the two women transformed into food trees.

A pedestrian with a CQ of 95.5, who had overheard the verbal exchange, scurried over to Kara.

"You're an elevator person," she said. "Touch me. Don't let me die."

"I'm sorry," Kara replied. "I can't save you."

"Then why are you wasting my time?" The pedestrian left in a huff.

&

Kara once again caught a glimpse of the black-and-purple kitten and continued the pursuit. Eventually, she caught up with the feline and told her, "I'm naming you Amy."

Kara carried the cat down a residential street, a shortcut back to the park. They came upon an elderly man named Jake with a CQ of 55.7; he was sweeping the front porch of his townhouse.

In his second-floor window, there were two birds in a cage.

"Hello, sir," Kara said.

"Good day," Jake replied.

"I'm not sure if you've heard, but everyone is gonna die within the next four days."

"I've heard that rumor." Jake continued sweeping. "It's not true."

"Well, it *is* true, and it's important you release your animals, so they have a chance at life."

"The rumor's hogwash. And I don't have any animals."

"Whose birds are those?" Kara pointed at the second-floor window.

"They belong to my roommate."

"I think we should release them now so they don't starve to death in their cage."

"They're not mine, and they're just birds." Jake sounded peeved.

Kara moved onto the porch next to him. "We wouldn't want them to suffer and die."

"They're just birds, lady." Jake looked at Kara like she was a loon. "And they don't belong to me."

"You may not realize this, but pain and death on Earth cause dangerous weather problems for other planets."

"That's a nutty theory." Jake gently pushed Kara. "Excuse me. You're in my way."

He tried to sweep around her feet.

"Oh, sorry." She backed up.

Jake continued to sweep, pretending his demented visitor was not there.

Kara stepped off the porch and started to leave, but then turned and again looked up at the birds. She returned to the townhouse.

"I wasn't gonna tell you this. But if you don't save the birds, you'll go to hell. This is judgment day, sir."

"I'm not a Christian," Jake replied.

"It's not about that. It's about being smart. What do you have to lose by freeing the birds? After all, they're just birds. If

I'm wrong, I've wasted a few minutes of your time. If I'm right, you've saved your soul for the rest of eternity."

Jake stared at Kara as she strutted away.

"The more animals you save, the more perks you'll get in heaven. But maybe you don't care if God likes you."

When Kara got a reasonable distance away, she turned to see Jake at the second-story window. He opened the cage, and the birds flew away.

❦

Kara rushed back to the park with Amy. She was enthusiastic because she had just figured out the secret to changing hearts and minds, or at least gaining a modicum of compliance with Bones's directive.

"Okay." Kara placed Amy on the table. "This save-the-world thing isn't gonna be as easy as we thought, but I've got an idea on how we can free the animals. Besides Miles, who's in?"

"I hope it doesn't involve going door-to-door," Bernie said. "Because that would take way more than a week."

"Charity people should work for a cause. Not applause," Ellen said. "So, I'm a green light."

Amy walked over to Roger and nuzzled him.

"Aw. How cute." Kara smiled. "She remembers you."

"You know I'm willing to help." Roger embraced the feline. "It's not like I have anything else to do."

"Teamwork's the key to success, ma'am, and I'm no slacker." Carl saluted Kara.

"What about you, Bernie?" Kara said. "Have you reconsidered?"

"I was always a yes."

Suddenly, there was honking in the distance. It was Angus in the driver's seat of a bright red Rolls Royce.

"Look at that showstopper," Carl said, as he and everyone, except Kara and Roger, headed to the vehicle.

"So, what's your plan?" Roger took a sip of orange juice.

"Ever heard of Pascal's Wager?" Kara asked. "You know… invented by the seventeenth-century philosopher Blaise Pascal?"

"No. Maybe you can explain it in plain English for those of us who haven't memorized the encyclopedia."

"The bottom line is this… Starting today, we are divine entities with a special connection to God. We're in the soul-saving business, Mr. Adams."

"We're gonna be Bible thumpers?"

⚘

The others were crowded around the Rolls Royce.

"Like my new wheels?" Angus beamed.

"Where'd you get it?" Keiko asked.

"Some dude turned into a tree. It's mine now. Let's go drag racing."

"I'm gonna stay," Keiko replied. "I'm not gonna let the victims starve."

"What the fuck's the matter with you?" Angus roared. "Dad always said you were soft. It's nauseating. I'm going out with a bang."

"I'm up for a bang." Bailey climbed into the vehicle.

"Bailey, what are you doing?" Ellen exclaimed.

"The universe screwed up my life so it can turn into a ham sandwich for all I care."

"See you, suckers." Angus grinned, and the car zoomed away.

⚘

The Pascal's Wager ploy, also known as the what-have-you-got-to-lose campaign, was in full swing. Roger and Kara hit the talk show circuit, giving interviews to every possible outlet. Producers were all too willing to book them as guests because they were coming out of the spaceship, so to speak. They were admitting they were elevator people.

No other vate in the world had made a public confession, except for a few folks in prison.

The interviews with Kara and Roger were drawing millions of eyeballs and generating high ratings for media outlets.

By this time, most members of the public were in a full-blown panic. It was universally accepted that people were turning into trees. Many individuals had witnessed at least one or two transitions—of strangers, friends, or sometimes family members.

In addition to personal accounts, the topic was increasingly discussed on TV and in the editorial pages of newspapers throughout the world. The prevailing view was that elevator people were causing the deaths—a belief that sprang from the fact that the arrival of the vates was concurrent with the "tree phenomenon." Politicians, journalists, and the masses were confusing causation with correlation.

They also thought the vates were sorcerers. The public not only thought elevator people were somehow magically inducing the bizarre modifications but were certain that these aliens could stop the insanity with the wave of a wand. Oddly, this gave the elevator people power. There was no longer an appetite for arresting and killing these extraterrestrial visitors; there was a desire to get on their good side.

Kara sat on a couch at a television studio next to a popular talk show host. Behind them was a backdrop. Lighting hung from the ceiling; there were microphones, cameras, a sound booth, and crew members.

"I'm here with Baltimore elevator person Dr. Kara Carson."

The host spoke into a camera and then faced her guest. "Dr. Carson, this is a devastating time. Many people have lost their loved ones, and they fear for their own lives. There's a rumor that you and the other vates caused these deaths, but you can also stop them. Is this true?"

"We didn't cause this, and we can't stop it," Kara said. "But we've spoken with the Supreme Being's deputy. He gave us a message to pass on."

"What's that?"

"Free the animals. People can avoid eternal suffering by freeing the animals."

"Free the animals? What do you mean?"

"People must go up and down the streets. Dogs, cats, birds, gerbils, turtles. Release any animal that could become trapped. Take freshwater fish to a lake and saltwater fish to the ocean. If you work at a pet store or research lab, you need to open the cages. If you work at a farm, you need to open the gates. Save your soul before it's too late."

"A lot of our viewers don't believe in God or a Supreme Being, Dr. Carson."

"It's okay if you don't believe. And it doesn't matter if you call him God, Allah, Brahma, Buddha, the Creator, or the father of the Big Bang. Or maybe it's a she, and she's the mother of the Big Bang. The bottom line is, you have nothing to lose by freeing the animals. It only requires a few minutes of your time. Don't take the risk. Be smart. You don't want to burn in hell."

"Are you saying everyone is destined to die?"

"Yes. Within the next few days. This is judgment day."

"There must be a way to stop the dying." The host looked mortified.

"No. Nothing can be done. But the afterlife can be paradise if you do the right thing now."

The free-the-animals campaign became the focus on every

continent. Vates around the world began to go public with their status as elevator people. They embraced the crusade, saying, "What have you got to lose?"

Creative billboards popped up. One in Hollywood, California read "Free the Animals. Share a Latte with God."

A placard in the U.K. read "Dear Brits, Free the Animals. Or Have a Bloody Bad Time in Hell."

In addition to doing publicity, Miles, Kara, Roger, Carl, Ellen, Bernie, and Keiko hit the pavement; they opened doors, cages, and windows. They traveled up and down the streets. They were pleased to see that most residents were helping with the mission.

There were reports of good deeds occurring far and wide. Grocery store clerks took lobsters to the ocean. The Happy Farms guards, Kip and Pete, unlatched the gates at several slaughterhouses. The animals at the Baltimore Zoo were liberated. Doors and windows were left ajar at residential properties. A capital "V," which stood for "vate," was scribbled on the side of completed buildings so others would know to move on to the next structure.

❧

It was the day before Kara's impending death. She was heading back to Miles's house after releasing six roosters from a backyard; they had been used as entertainment in the blood sport of cockfighting.

She came upon the Worthington Research Institute, where she saw the shrubbery that was once Olive and Dr. Dijon. It was obvious due to the placement of the "Research Grant" folder on the sidewalk. A lion, two rabbits, and a songbird peacefully nibbled on the tree that had once been her cruel boss.

Kara couldn't believe it! The very same tree! These two women had spent their adult lives as "Angels of Death," causing pain and functioning as executioners. Finally, they were help-ing other creatures. Nice had replaced vice. A loving shift had replaced a malignant rift. Empathy had replaced misery. Kara was pleased. The planet had transformed into a Shangri-la.

Chapter Sixteen

DYSTOPIA OR UTOPIA?

It was less than sixty minutes before the witching hour, also known as death. Miles and all the vates, except Angus and Bailey, were in the living room eating salad, French bread, and key lime pie, which they called their "last supper." They wondered whether the new world would qualify as a utopia.

Kara pulled out a dictionary to review the official definition and etymology for the term. She explained that the word was coined in 1516 by Sir Thomas More and came from the Greek for "no" and "place."

"Utopia is usually related to laws, government, and social conditions." Kara studied the reference book. "It describes a perfect society in which people work well with each other and are happy."

"Do you see the flaw in that definition?" Miles asked.

"I do." Kara smiled. "It's centered around humans. It implies there can't be a perfect world without people."

Miles clapped.

"Postmodern deconstruction is an important tool of analysis," Kara added, and then she looked up the term "dystopia." "It's an imagined world or society in which people lead wretched, dehumanized, fearful lives."

"That's got the same dang problem. Fool me once. The only person who ever fooled me twice was a boy named Johnny Twice." Carl chuckled.

Miles's cruelty quotient had nose-dived down to zero and remained there for three days. Ellen brought attention to it, calling Miles "The most perfect person on the planet."

"I wonder if your number would go up if you punch someone," Keiko said.

"Buddhism teaches that you can be violent with words," Ellen offered. "So maybe your score would shoot up if you say something hateful."

"Let's give it a try. Yell at me," Bernie suggested.

"No. I want to die with zero."

"Bet you'll be the only dude to ever croak with a goose egg." Carl laughed.

While the vates were in the living room engaging in philosophy, Angus and Bailey were playing pinball and watching a movie in the basement. They seemed oblivious to the fact that their demise was less than an hour away.

Bailey wore a blue bow in her hair, which Angus had gifted her. It was his version of a promise ring. He'd told her that a diamond was a little more commitment than he felt comfortable with.

Rather than rescuing animals, Angus and Bailey spent the week swimming, dancing, drag racing, boating, singing karaoke, and consuming large quantities of alcohol. They also embarked on a romantic relationship. They had come back to Miles's house for one reason: it had a groovy game room.

The vates in the living room could hear periodic dings and whistles from the pinball machine, as well as sporadic shouts of delight by the twosome as they won and lost points.

Kara floated an observation. "It's interesting how we were hated and feared. Then we were seen as saviors."

"For a species that prides itself on intelligence, it sure is full of idiots," Bernie quipped.

"I think when people got scared, they didn't want to see us as the enemy," Kara added. "They needed to have hope. We represented that hope."

Roger turned to Kara. "You're beautiful *and* insightful."

"Wow. Thank you, Roger. And I'm not even wearing my Wet n Wild lip gloss."

Suddenly, the vates heard a crash. They rushed into the kitchen to find that a tree branch had blasted through a window. Plants had sprouted all over the room, and vines were coiled up in Miss Pringles's animal bed. It resembled a canine topiary; the bed had flowers for eyes.

Everyone made their way to the front yard, and they were shocked to find greenery covering almost the entire façade of the house.

"I wonder if State Farm insures mountains," Carl joked.

Miles checked his watch. "It's gonna happen soon. Let's go back inside."

Kara, Roger, Ellen, Carl, Keiko, and Bernie made their way to the living room while Miles opened windows and doors for the pigs, the beagles, Angel, and Amy.

Miles grabbed a glass of wine and settled on the couch. Sammy and Miss Pringles placed their heads in his lap. The other animals were present. Angel was cuddled up next to Kara.

Miles consulted his watch. "We've got fifteen minutes."

"I'm in the fourth stage of grief," Ellen said. "I don't think I'll make it to acceptance before noon."

"Me neither." Kara kissed the top of Angel's head.

"This whole thing isn't fair," Bernie complained.

"Try to look at the bright side," Miles said.

"We don't want to look at the bright side, Miles," Roger replied. "We want to wallow in our grief."

"Fine." Miles took a sip of wine.

"Why isn't the sudden death of humans causing monsoons and drought on other planets?" Ellen asked.

"Maybe cause people are not really dying," Kara replied. "They're transforming into another life form."

There was an awkward silence. The vates sat stiff and emotionless, awaiting death.

Miles examined his watch again. "It's five minutes till noon."

"Will you tell me when I turn into a tree?" Kara asked.

"I don't think you'll be conscious," Roger said.

"*The Secret Life of Plants* says trees are conscious," Kara added.

"What do you think will happen after we die?" Keiko inquired.

"I believe in reincarnation." Ellen stroked one of the beagles. "I just hope I don't come back as an asshole with a sky-high cruelty quotient."

"I think there's a heaven, and God's happy we saved so many animals," Bernie said.

"If I turn into a tree first, will you make sure little Angel doesn't get caught in my branches?" Kara wept.

Roger moved over to comfort her.

Ellen and Bernie broke into tears, and the vates joined together for a group hug.

Suddenly everyone heard that devastating noise. It was the sound of whales moaning, followed by breaking bones. It was coming from the basement.

Keiko jumped up in a panic and ran downstairs, where he found two food trees next to the pinball machine. There was a blue ribbon tied around one of the branches. He wailed in anguish.

"I think Angus and Bailey went to that Giant Sequoia in the sky," Roger said solemnly.

Miles broke away from the group hug and glanced down at his watch. "It's 12:02. Why aren't we dead?"

"I don't know," Kara replied.

"Maybe they forgot about us," Bernie guessed.

"Or maybe it takes time to get through 362,000 people," Ellen said. "We might be scheduled for 12:30 or 12:45."

❧

It was three p.m. The vates were in the living room.

"This is ridiculous," Kara shouted. "We should be dead by now."

"Why is it taking so long?" Ellen exclaimed. "Now I have to go to the bathroom."

"It's just too stressful," Kara said. "It needs to happen already."

"The Council with their fat beaks is totally incompetent," Ellen blurted out.

"I bet that troublemaker, Sheldon, has something to do with it," Kara stated.

There were sighs and expressions of frustration from everyone, except Miles and Carl, who were napping.

❧

Hours passed. It was 8:30 p.m. The vates were flipping through magazines, reading books, eating snacks, and reclining in various positions on couches and armchairs.

"Okay. That's it." Kara jumped up. "I'm sorry, but I need to know what's going on."

"What do you mean?" Bernie asked.

"I need to talk to Bones."

"No," Bernie pleaded. "They probably forgot about us."

"I'm not going to bed without knowing whether I'm gonna wake up an American woman or a Spanish oak." Kara walked toward the door.

"I agree." Roger stood.

"Who wants to come with us?" Kara asked.

"No." Bernie tackled Kara's legs to stop her from leaving.

∾

The Zelles Hotel was almost entirely covered in plants. Kara and Roger felt around for the glass entrance, then broke through it with a metal rod.

The elevator doors were also covered in greenery. Roger fumbled around until he found the call button, which he pushed again and again.

Nothing happened.

The vates waited five minutes; then they started pounding on the lift doors.

"Bones?" Kara screamed. "Where are you?"

"Open up," Roger yelled. "Let us in."

"We need to talk to you, Bones," Kara hollered. "It's urgent."

After a great deal of banging and yelling, the doors opened. The interior of the elevator was covered almost entirely in plants. It looked dangerous. Kara and Roger were reluctant to get inside but did so anyway.

Roger pushed the button for the fiftieth floor. The lift shook, squealed, jolted, and went through its usual shenanigans as it headed upward. The vates held on to vegetation for stability.

When they reached level 50, Roger pushed the "up" button, and the elevator climbed to the fifty-first floor. The doors slid open, and Bones appeared.

"Thank goodness," Kara said. "There you are."

"Hello, tourists. You're lucky I was on the planet." Bones peered into the elevator and flashed a look of horror. "Yikes. This is the last time I'm visiting this elevator. It's totally falling apart. Okay. What's so urgent?"

"We're confused because we didn't die at noon," Kara replied.

"We don't want to go through life wondering if we're gonna turn into food trees," Roger said.

"Not knowing is too stressful," Kara admitted.

"I'm happy to report… the Council made an exception based on your excellent scores. You passed your empathy exam, and your free-the-animals campaign… . Well, that was nothing short of Einstein-level genius."

"Really? Einstein?" Kara blushed. "Well, I don't know about that. Maybe I'm a little like Einstein. Of course, he—"

"Kara," Roger interrupted, holding his finger up to his lips. "Shhh." Then he turned to Bones. "So, we're not gonna die?"

"Not unless the elevator plummets to the ground."

The floating board materialized next to Bones. Gibberish appeared on it at supersonic speed.

"And based on my calculation, there's a 73.2 percent chance the elevator will plummet to the ground," Bones said.

"What?" Kara and Roger spoke in unison.

The board disappeared, and Bones laughed. "I'm just kidding. I made that up."

"Are we the only people who didn't die?" Roger asked.

"Nope. Negative. Well, toodle-oo, tourists. I'm gonna miss

trying to avoid you." Bones vanished, but then immediately reappeared. "Oops. I almost forgot. And this is very, very important. You're not elevator people. You're *elevated* people. Never forget that."

With that, he disappeared, and the doors slammed shut.

❧

It was the next morning. Plants had engulfed a significant portion of roadways, lawns, and buildings. It was as if nature was determined to erase every trace of human existence. Birds sang and myriad animals ate from food trees.

Ellen, Bernie, Carl, Keiko, and Miles strolled down a street next to the pocket park in the town square, checking out barely identifiable shops and eateries. They saw a rusty gun and a corroded cage near a pet store. They peeked into an antique shop to find a woodpecker striking a grandfather clock. A pig and her babies were nestled on a costly canopy bed.

"The only real charity work I ever did was this war on cruelty," Ellen admitted. "Everything else was virtue signaling. I know that now."

"I wasn't brave enough to finish my grandmother's work until you guys came along," Miles said. "I was hiding in my basement like a lost sock."

The vates saw a food tree growing through the broken window of a Mercedes. Small dogs were huddled together in the open trunk of the car, and a family of large dogs were nestled in the passenger section. Next to the car was a Gucci loafer inhabited by baby mice. And nearby was an open Tory Burch handbag; a colony of rabbits had made a home inside.

The vates peered through the window of a fine jewelry store, filled with an assortment of plants. A bird had constructed a nest for her babies in the corner, using sticks, leaves, grass, diamonds, and rubies.

"Hey, Miles," Ellen asked. "Did the underground give you any information about where we might find other elevator people?"

"I've got a list where they were spotted. The closest is the Hilton in Alexandria, Virginia."

"We should go there and see if anyone's alive," Bernie suggested.

"Great idea," Keiko said. "Let's build up civilization and fuck up the world all over again."

Everyone stared at Keiko, dumbfounded.

"I'm kidding." He laughed. "I'm just kidding, I promise."

"Alexandria's about an hour by car," Miles said.

Carl pointed at an abandoned helicopter parked on a street in the distance. "It's only thirty minutes by Apache. They don't call me the Whirlybird Wagon Master for nothing. Be back in a jiffy."

He bolted toward the chopper.

"Poor old man," Bernie said. "He thinks he can fly a helicopter."

A few minutes later, Miles, Bernie, Ellen, and Keiko were amazed to see the helicopter in the air with Carl waving from the cockpit.

"Save me a couple of branches for dinner," he shouted as he flew out of sight.

&

Kara and Roger were in the pocket park with the animals. Angel, the pigs, and the beagles frolicked on the grass. Amy, the cat, watched everyone from atop a picnic table.

Roger had his arm around Kara, and they sang "In the Year 2525" by Zager and Evans. They finished the final refrain of the song.

"Did you know the largest living organism on the planet is

in Utah?" Kara said. "It's a forest made up of 47,000 trees with a single root system."

"Hey…" Roger acted surprised. "What's that writing on your chest?"

"Oh, my gosh! Do I have a cruelty quotient?"

"No. It says 'Beauty quotient: 100. Extreme Caution!'"

"Ahh, you're such a sweet guy."

"You can thank my inner tree. Sometimes it gets all sappy."

In the end, Bones was a hero, the Council was pleased… and the Earth and its inhabitants—including the elevated people— were finally at peace.

"Charlotte Laws is unquestionably a maverick.… [Her writing] is a page-turner…"

Atlanta Jewish Times

"Dr. Laws is a champion of the underdog."

New York Post

"Charlotte Laws is a tenacious bulldog when she latches onto something."

Atlanta Journal-Constitution

"Laws is a woman of many talents… [and] a hero."

Newsweek

Author Biography

Charlotte Laws is an award-winning and bestselling writer. She has authored seven books, contributed to four academic anthologies, and written 135 articles that have appeared in various publications, including the *Washington Post*, the *Los Angeles Times*, *Newsweek*, *Salon*, *Huffington Post*, and the *New York Daily News*.

Laws has a Ph.D. in Social Ethics from the University of Southern California, two master's degrees, and two BA degrees. She completed her postdoctoral study at Oxford University, England.

Laws was a Greater Valley Glen Councilmember for eight years and currently stars in the Netflix series *The Most Hated Man on the Internet*. She worked as a pundit on BBC television and the NBC show *The Filter*. She has appeared on CNN, *The Late Show*, Fox News, *Oprah*, *Larry King Live*, MSNBC, and *Nightline*, and has been featured in the *New York Times*, the *San Francisco Chronicle*, and the *Guardian*.

She is a recipient of the Los Angeles Animal Humanitarian Award and lives in Los Angeles with her husband, her two rescue dogs, and her five rescue hens.